'Don't Evy

He smiled te[...]
apprehensio[...]?'

'Kissing me.'

'I wasn't. I was thinking about doing a lot more than kissing.' He bent, tucking a finger under her chin and tipping up her face. His mouth was a fraction away from hers.

Delicious tremors swept through her, making her insides heavy with want. Hayley was tempted but self-preservation and old hurt won out. She pressed a hand to his lips, halting him. His gaze swept to hers.

'Don't, this will lead to nowhere but heartache.' She was surprised she managed to get the words past her lips with him looking at her like that. 'And I've been there.'

Nash realised the magnitude of what he was doing and eased back. He thought he saw disappointment in her eyes, but he couldn't be sure…

Dear Reader

Welcome to June's selection of six breathtaking Desires™.

Popular writer Barbara Boswell returns with *Bachelor Doctor*, where we wonder if sexy surgeon Dr Trey Weldon really can say goodbye to bachelor life. We have two gorgeous grooms in Peggy Moreland's *In Name Only* and Amy J Fetzer's *Wife for Hire*. And there's another hero lining up to be husband *and* a daddy in Metsy Hingle's *The Baby Bonus* where the couple make a remarriage of convenience...

Jennifer Greene's *Rock Solid* is a spicy tale of love and passion in our BODY AND SOUL promotion—it'll really get the temperature soaring, we can promise you that!

Finally, we are delighted to bring you the final instalment of our exciting mini-series ROYALLY WED. *A Royal Mission* by Elizabeth August is the breathtaking tale of a handsome hero rescuing a *very* special damsel in distress!

All the best,

The Editors

Wife for Hire

AMY J FETZER

SILHOUETTE
DESIRE®

*Silhouette, Silhouette Desire and Colophon
are registered trademarks of Harlequin Books S.A.,
used under licence.*

*First published in Great Britain 2001
Silhouette Books, Eton House, 18-24 Paradise Road,
Richmond, Surrey TW9 1SR*

© Amy J Fetzer 2000

ISBN 0 373 76305 0

22-0601

*Printed and bound in Spain
by Litografía Rosés S.A., Barcelona*

AMY J FETZER

was born in New England and raised all over the world. She uses her own experiences in creating the characters and settings for her novels. Married nineteen years to a United States Marine, and the mother of two sons, Amy covets the moments when she can curl up with a cup of cappuccino and a good book.

For my friend and publicist,
Terri Farrell.

For pep talks via e-mail, Godiva
and slugging through some of the worst titles in
recorded history. For those clever ideas and keeping
on top of my promotion so I focus on my writing.
For those little surprises that arrive when I need them
the most. For making me always feel important, and
your quirky sense of humour. You've been a
tremendous help, Ter.

Now aren't you glad I talked you into this job?

Thanks.

One

River Willow Plantation
Aiken, South Carolina

She had a rubber chicken stuck in the grillwork of her car.

The webbed feet flopped with every bump, the chicken looking as if it was being strangled and fried for supper, with all the smoke coming from the exhaust.

Nash Rayburn's lips twitched with amusement. "At least she has a sense of humor," he muttered to himself, then glanced down at his daughters. They were grinning widely. A good sign, he thought, nudging his hat back and bracing his shoulder on the porch post. He hooked his thumbs in his belt loops.

This was his wife for hire?

The dust-covered car rattled to a stop about twenty

yards away and choked for a full twenty seconds after she shut the engine off and climbed out. Nash felt an instant pull in his gut the moment shapely bare legs first appeared and touched the ground.

Strike one. She was pretty. No, downright adorable, reminding him of a fairy in a story his mama told him when he was a kid. Her eyes hidden behind dark sunglasses, she had gleaming short dark-red hair and a body that was graceful and voluptuous. That pull tightened in places he didn't want to acknowledge.

Strike two.

He'd told the agency he didn't want anyone who'd distract the ranch hands. Now a petite full-breasted slim-hipped woman was coming straight toward him. And her Cadillac walk was so sexy he had the urge to cover his daughters' eyes. Damn. A scoop-neck navy blue T-shirt, a short denim skirt and a pair of high heeled sandals had never looked that good on his late wife.

"Oh, goody, she's not old," Kim said as if it was a crime to be over ten. "She can play games with us."

Nash glanced down at his twin girls. "Mrs. Winslow plays games."

The two made faces at him. "Board games and stuff. She just watches us mostly," Kate said, looking at the woman. "She looks nice, huh, Daddy?"

Breathtaking, he thought, and hoped his voice didn't show it. "Yes, peanut, very nice."

Ten yards away, the woman's steps slowed to a stop, and Nash felt suddenly uneasy, a sense of familiarity hitting him. His gaze swept over her, searching for a connection.

"Nash?"

His blood froze and he straightened. He'd know that

voice anywhere. Hayley Albright. *His* Hayley. "What are you doing here?"

She cocked one hip, her fingers tightening on the strap of a beat-up leather handbag slung on her shoulder. "If this is Katherine's idea of a joke, I don't like it."

"Me, neither." Nash's insides twisted, his heart pressing against his ribs. Seven years ago he'd loved this woman. And seven years ago he'd betrayed that love and married another. He could never tell her why. Never. Yet one look at her and every cell in his body reacted, screaming for her. His blood grew hot and heavy in his veins as he stepped off the porch, walking toward her. It had always been like that, so good it was almost painful to be near her. She was the kind of woman who made heads turn as much for her confidence as for her beauty. The kind who made you smile just because she smiled.

The kind he'd wanted to marry.

Hayley felt memories of her past flow back as he neared, meshing with the old pain. She tried to push them aside, tried to gather her composure, but he was looking at her the way he had years ago. As if he wanted to devour her whole. It made her knees weak. She wanted to turn back to her car and drive away to avoid opening this part of her past again. It hurt too much. When he approached and stopped directly in front of her, the urge to throw herself into his arms made her eyes sting. It made her see that even if she told herself she was over him, she wasn't. Not by a long shot. Out of sight didn't mean out of mind—or heart. And if she stayed, she'd be in trouble.

Then he plucked off her sunglasses.

She snatched them back and met his gaze head on, searching for the man she once loved.

"You're working for Katherine's company?"

"A girl's got to make a living."

His lips flattened to a thin line. "What about your dream to be a doctor?"

She hitched up her handbag and said, "Still there. I just finished my internship. After a two-week break, I'll go back to St. Anthony's Hospital to begin my residency."

"That's great." His smile was slight, bitter, and Hayley felt as if she'd been kicked in the stomach. Her need to be a doctor and his need to have her abandon her goal in order to be his wife had torn holes in their love and sent him into the arms of another woman.

"Somehow I don't think that's what you really mean," she said.

His gaze narrowed. "I never wanted you to fail, Hayley."

"No, just dump my dreams for yours."

His features yanked taut. This conversation was just too difficult for public discussion, for what he was feeling, what he wanted to say to her. What he wanted to do with her. He caught the scent of jasmine, feeling it sing through his veins and make him ache to hold her. "It *is* good to see you."

The low tone of his voice evoked heat and the sensation of being safely wrapped in warmth. "Good to be seen," she managed and searched his face for any changes. They were minor, for he'd aged beautifully, the lines in his face giving it more character, a harder look than she remembered. At thirty-five he was as handsome as he was when she'd first seen him at a college mixer in her senior year. He'd arrived with his friend Katherine Davenport, Hayley's sorority sister, mentor and owner of Wife Incorporated, just as a favor, and he'd left with Hayley. He was the older man, rich and powerful, who'd swept her off her feet and into his strong capable arms. She sighed, pushing the memory down where it belonged. She'd been a fool, falling for him hook, line and sinker, and she wasn't about to let it happen again.

They stared at each other for a moment longer before Hayley asked the one question she didn't want to say. "So, where's Michelle?"

His features hardened. "She'd dead, Hayley. Killed in a car accident four years ago."

"I'm sorry." She was. Hayley might have a grudge against Michelle and Nash, but she certainly didn't wish his wife dead.

"You know her, Daddy?" a voice asked.

Hayley stepped away and looked at the girls standing on the porch. While her assignment sheet offered only a street address, not a name—which she'd rail at Kat later for omitting—the job was detailed and she'd expected children. She smiled and waved. "Oh, Nash," she said softly, in a tone full of surprise. "They look just like you."

He didn't take his eyes off her, enjoying her unrestrained smile. "I don't know if that's good or bad."

She glanced. "Good," she said honestly as the twins trotted down the wide Federal steps and flanked their father.

"These two beauties," he said, ruffling the top of one dark head, "are Kim and Kate."

"I'm Hayley," she said, and shook their little hands. "And yes, your daddy and I are old friends." She gave them a conspiratorial wink that made the five-year-olds giggle.

Nash felt the tension leave her body as if he owned her skin, and he was glad that any animosity she had for him didn't spill over to his girls. How were they going to work this out? How long could he stand having her in his house, living with him, seeing her every day and knowing she hated him? It was a humiliation he'd continue to bear in silence. Keeping the truth from her would keep any feelings from being resurrected, he decided. And asking her to leave would be his best bet.

She swung her gaze to his, tipped her head to the side as if studying a painting. Her lips curved into a soft smile that caught him in the gut and threatened the seams of his anger.

Hayley sensed it and frowned. What did he have to be so mad about? She was the one who was jilted, while he'd had everything he wanted. A beautiful wife with culture, wealth and the same refinement he possessed. A perfect complement to the rich powerful landowner he'd become. "I can see you're not happy about this," she said, "so how about I call Kat and have another wife for hire here by morning?"

His eyes flared. The challenge was there. Nash had to admire her for it. Even when he wanted her gone. Just seeing her made his mistakes more pronounced. They felt like a knife in his side, and every time their eyes met, it twisted.

"Did you like our daddy?" one of the twins interjected.

Their curiosity was open and charming, yet Hayley could feel their father tense, feel his eyes on her as she looked down at the girls. "I thought he was the handsomest man on earth."

The twins giggled again, huddling closer. Nash glanced down and their smiles fell a little. He supposed he deserved their retreat with the way he'd been barking at them all week; but Mrs. Winslow was off sick, and he had hundreds of horses, cattle, pigs, chickens and two brunette mischief makers roaming where they weren't supposed to. Plus he'd had all his other duties to attend to. Bless their hearts, he loved his babies, but they were a full-time job. He eyed Hayley, wondering if she could keep up with his pair of tornadoes.

"I can handle the situation," Nash said. "Can you?"

The challenge was there, she thought. He should know better than to dare her. "No sweat."

"Fine," he said, then turned and walked toward the house.

"Ooh, attitude already."

He paused and looked back at her, arching a dark brow. She smiled brightly, motioning for him to lead the way. The twins were already stuck to her side and sharing secrets. Great. Outnumbered already, he thought sourly, pushing open the front door. He stepped into the coolness of the house, the girls skipping past him into the den and clicking on the television.

He tossed his hat onto the side table and ran his fingers through his dark hair. "Turn it down a notch, will you, girls?" They did as he asked without a look back.

Nash stared down at Hayley, watching her gaze move over the foyer, the large open living room beyond, the furnishings, then to the left to the hall leading to the bedrooms and second floor. To the right lay a combination kitchen, dining area and den, or what real-estate agents called a Carolina room, and he searched her expression for a reaction, then wondered why he bothered.

She brought her gaze back to his. "Nice digs, Nash."

He eyed her. "Thanks."

"So, what's first?"

He inclined his head toward the kitchen. "What did the agency tell you?" he said as he walked.

"That you needed a temporary wife and all-around kid wrangler for two little girls."

He stilled and snapped a black look back over his shoulder. "I don't need a wife."

Hayley blinked, frowning. "I was speaking figuratively, Nash."

His gaze swept over her thoroughly, and she stared back, dropping her hand to her hip and waiting for him to continue. *This ought to be good,* she thought.

"The plantation needs a cook and housekeeper, and my daughters need supervision. Household chores are Mrs. Winslow's and now they're yours. The girls have chores, too. The list is on the fridge." He faced her. "This is temporary, and if I could manage without help, I would. Understand?"

"Quite well, as a matter of fact." There was no room in his life for her other than as the domestic help, and he'd just made it crystal clear.

"And the cooking is for seven ranch hands, too."

She shrugged. "Two, five, ten, it doesn't matter. As long as there's food to prepare."

He eyed her skeptically. "I don't recall you being much of a cook."

"A lot has changed in seven years, Nash."

Her mysterious smile set him on edge, and the question about where she'd been, what she'd been doing besides graduate study, nagged at him. But he was determined to keep this relationship strictly business. Even if she was still sexy enough to make his jeans feel crowded.

"I guess we'll get to see that, won't we?" His words snapped off with the bite of lash.

She frowned. This wasn't the Nash she remembered. This man was hard on the inside, apparently, as well as the outside. He never once smiled and he was the epitome of tall, dark and brooding. She half expected him to whip out a sword, draw a line in the carpet and dare her to cross it. His stare was intense, deep blue—and having far too powerful an effect on her.

"No, taste it." Her brow knit. "If you doubt me, then why did you agree to have me stay?"

"I'm short on time and you're here."

"Gee. Thanks for throwing a bone my way."

Nash sighed and ran his fingers through his hair again. How was he going to last two weeks when he all he wanted to do was kiss her senseless? "I didn't mean it that way."

"Look, Nash. We have a past and it's over and dead. You have no real reason to be upset with me..." She let the sentence hang, implying that she alone had reason. "If I'm going to work for you, don't you think you could cut me some slack?"

His gaze darkened, raked her with the same heat as when she first saw him. She ought to be immune to a look like that. She wasn't. It didn't help that it was hidden in anger, or that she had to crane her neck to look up at him, making her feel like a shrimp in an ocean of sharks. Or that he filled out that black T-shirt rather well after all these years. And for a split second she remembered what he looked like without a stitch.

Uh-oh, this was not in her plan, she thought, trying to focus as he described duties and meal preferences. He moved through the large kitchen to the laundry room, which was stacked with soiled clothes, then back around into the Carolina room. Pausing to check on what his daughters were watching on TV, he headed toward the hall. She followed.

"My office, and off-limits." He gestured without looking back at her.

"Aye, aye, Captain."

He cast her a sharp glance. She blinked sweetly and motioned for him to proceed.

He walked, pointing out the steep staircase leading to the girls' rooms on the second floor, informing her that Mrs. Winslow went home to her son's each evening unless work took Nash into the night. He stopped before a door, turned the knob, pushed, then leaned back against the frame, waiting.

"Your room."

She looked. It was a normal guest bedroom, neutral decor, bright with sunlight. Was he waiting for her to disapprove of something? She hadn't had a room to call her own until college, but walls meant little to Hayley; it was what was inside them that mattered. "This is fine." She hurled her bag onto the bed, kicked off her shoes and looked at him. Wonderful. He was now another two inches taller.

"I suppose you have work to do. I'll get started." She walked back down the hall.

Nash blinked and straightened. "Don't you need...?"

She glanced over her shoulder, enjoying his confusion. "What? More instructions? That's not why you hired me. The agency gave me a thorough job description. Go do whatever it is you do on a horse ranch or plantation or whatever." She waved toward the door as she walked into the living room. "We'll be fine. Won't we, girls?"

The twins spun on the sofa, peering over the back of it like squirrels. Hayley winked. They were button cute and itching with energy they'd obviously learned to curtail around their dad. Their gazes shifted to him, then to her.

"Would you like me to fix you some lunch or something before you go?" Hayley asked Nash.

"No." Nash had the feeling he was being dismissed in his own house. "Chow's usually at sundown."

"It'll be ready."

His look said he doubted that as he grabbed his hat, eyed her briefly, then crossed to the sofa, sinking between his daughters and pulling them onto his lap. "I wish I could hang around with you." He made an exaggerated sad face and they giggled.

"Horses won't get fed," Kate said.

"Then they'll be too stubborn to sell," her sister added. "We'll be okay."

They were so grown-up about this, and Nash's chest tightened. "Behave. No mischief like yesterday."

They blushed. "Yup." He eyed them. "Yes, Daddy," they chimed.

"Promise?" He held up his little finger, and his daughters hooked theirs around his and nodded. He grinned, kissed them, then shifted them off his lap.

Hayley felt like the outsider she was and wished she'd been that close to her father at that age. She'd lost her mom when she was seven, and her father, being a salesman, dragged her all over the country. She met many people, saw wonderful sights, but never knew permanence, never had a home until the sorority house in college. If the twins weren't so cute she could almost envy them. They'd grown up in this house with the same people around them, and would probably marry local boys and have their weddings right here. Her heart jerked. Were Michelle and Nash married here? She warned herself not to go there. It was too painful to even ask. And it was the past. Why open up the wound?

Nash crossed to her and for a second he just stared, then said, "Those girls are my life, Hayley."

His heart was on his sleeve just then, and Hayley was touched by the depth of his feelings for his daughters. "I'll take good care of them, I promise," she said.

He nodded briskly and left.

Hayley sighed, a little too drained around that man. She looked at the girls. "There's a lot of work to do. So you can either sit there and watch TV for the next hour, fry a few more brain cells, or you can lend a hand and we'll have some fun later. Whaddaya say?"

"What kind of fun?"

Hayley looked thoughtful. "I think this should be a group decision."

They were off the sofa in less time than it took to take a breath, following her like mice to cheese.

"That your new wife, boss?"

Nash didn't respond to the ranch hand's comment and continued walking toward the barn, yanking his gloves from his back pocket.

"I thought mail-order brides went out in the nineteenth century," Seth snickered.

"Y'all must have your work done if you're sitting on your butts, right?" Nash said, pulling on the gloves.

Young Beau hopped off the back of the truck and hefted another hay bale onto the bed.

Nash paused long enough to issue orders before he strode into the breeding barn. The Thoroughbred auction was a week away, and his stock had better be in prime condition to sell. Briefly he checked on a mare about to foal, thinking how this addition was going to help stock his lands with good Thoroughbreds. Anyone for miles around this country knew it wasn't the horses a breeder had, but the land they had to graze and raise them. This land had been under the guardianship of a Rayburn since before the American Revolution, and Nash had always felt there were generations of his ancestors staring down at him the day he took over the reins. He had a reputation and tradition to maintain, but with the girls growing and needing more of him, it was getting harder to divide his time and do the things he needed to make their life better.

Nash muttered a curse and knew he was just avoiding any thoughts of Hayley. She still made him breathe hard, and he knew he hadn't been very congenial to her. It wasn't her fault he couldn't control his emotions around her. She stirred up every memory he'd suppressed since he'd broken up with her—and married Michelle.

Walking into the stall of the horse he usually rode, Nash saddled the animal. Then he paused with his hand on the pommel. He couldn't tell Hayley the truth, even if it was to ease the old hurt she tried to deny she felt. It would just make the entire situation worse. Mounting his horse, he rode around the rim of the paddock before leaping the fence and taking off across the pasture, trying hard not to think that the one woman he'd wanted in his house was now there. Or that his first honest, totally masculine reaction when he saw her was to wonder whether she still looked as good naked as she did fully clothed.

Hayley hefted the picnic basket, walking down the long stone-scattered driveway and heading off on the side road, under the drape of willow and sweet-gum trees, to the barns. Beside her, Kim and Kate each carried a big thermos and struggled to keep up. She veered in the direction of voices. Male voices. When she rounded the edge of the barn, she gave a shrill whistle, bringing heads around.

"Hey, fellas," she called, holding up the basket. "Hungry?"

Six men dropped their pitchforks, lashed leads to posts or set shovels aside and came to her like foxes after bunnies as she set the basket on the tailgate of the truck and opened the lid. She introduced herself and each ranch hand tipped his hat a fraction and nodded cordially. Jimmy Lee was long and lanky with a big smile and deeply tanned skin. He had an intense stare and wasn't above having a look-see of her from head to foot, until Beau nudged him. Beau was young, just out of high school, she imagined, and blushed went she shook his hand. There was Ronnie, about forty, with hair too long for his age and tied back in a ponytail, his straw cowboy hat crimped to fit his head just so. He didn't talk and just eyeballed her, accepting a cup of cold water. Then there was Bubba.

"Just what name does Bubba replace?" she asked the older man, gray-haired with weathered features and a sweat-dampened dark T-shirt.

"Robert. Bob."

Hayley decided Robert fit him better, despite the muscled chest, John Deere hat and overalls. Seth moved closer, lifting Kate and Kim onto the tailgate and peering into the basket.

"Miss Hayley made sandwiches, Mr. Seth. Big hulking ones," Kate said, glancing at Hayley.

She winked, then motioned to the twins with a stack of paper cups to pour some water for the men first. "I've got roast beef, ham and cheese, turkey and plenty of everything." Hayley fluffed out a tablecloth, then hitched her rear on the tailgate to lay out the meal with chips and fruit. "There's coffee for you, Ronnie," she said. "Kim mentioned you favored it, even in this heat."

"Yes, ma'am, I do." He took the thermos and poured a steaming cup.

Hayley felt perspiration trickle down her spine at just the thought of drinking it right now.

She served up a plateful for each of the men, then pulled out the peanut-butter-and-jelly sandwiches the girls had requested. Sitting atop hay bales in the truck, Kim and Kate were in heaven over the outdoor break. As she munched, Hayley studied the house. It was a massive structure in the low-country, two-story style, with a porch that wrapped completely around it. And this one, she'd discovered while vacuuming earlier, went on forever. There were six bedrooms in the place, and there was also a guest cottage out back near the pool. Beyond the two huge barns was a bunkhouse. The whole place was beautiful, and Hayley relaxed just looking at it. River Willow. She'd forgotten the name over the years, but as with Nash, that was all she'd forgotten.

The distant sound of hoofbeats came to Hayley, and she glanced around just as Nash came riding over the hill from the west side of the house. The girls waved and he waved back. He paused on the hill, shadowed beneath a tall willow tree, and her heart did a strange leap in her chest. That was just too much man for one body, she thought. He looked magnificent, exuding strength and masculine power, and for an instant, the image of a man, a hundred years ago in a billowy white shirt and knee breeches, flooded her mind. Old family, a Southern gentleman, even if he'd grown sharp around the edges. He met her gaze, and even at this distance she could feel it glide over her skin, pause where it shouldn't, yet flattering her that it did.

He still turns me inside out, she thought.

His horse pranced delicately before he bolted toward the barns. Hayley turned back to the truck, resisting the urge to fan herself. The girls wadded up the sandwich wrappers and tossed them in the basket. She sent them off to collect the trash from the men as she packed up. When she looked up again, Nash was a few yards away. But she'd heard him, felt her pulse quicken when she knew he was riding closer. It was disgusting, this chaos she felt around him still.

"What are you doing out here?" He slid from the horse's back and stormed toward her.

If he thought she'd run for cover, he was wrong. She had to stick with this, finish this job. And nothing, not even his intimidating glare, was going to make her back down. "Y'all need to stiffen up a bit." She gestured to the ranch hands and Nash. "You're just too loose and happy-go-lucky. I'm surprised you get a lick of work done." The hands snickered, moving quickly off, and Nash stopped, his blue eyes narrowing.

"Does it hurt?" she asked.

He looked at her from beneath the brim of his hat. "Does what hurt?"

"To smile."

Disarmed, his lips twitched. Behind her, the twins giggled.

"Guess not." Nash wondered now why he was so angry. Was it that his ranch hands were flirting with

her, or was it that she was simply here, winning everyone over but him?

"Thanks a heap, Miss Hayley," Jimmy Lee said as
he sauntered back, handing her his cup and letting his
gaze slide up and down long enough to make her blush.

"You're a rascal, Jim."

Nash gritted his teeth at the smile she gave the man.

"That's what my mama keeps saying."

He walked away and Hayley flipped open the basket
and held out a sandwich to Nash. "Would you like
one?"

He looked between her and the sandwich.

"This doesn't take a lot of brain power, Nash. A
simple yes or no will do."

Nash took the sandwich. She tossed him a soda, forc-
ing him to catch it.

"Come on, girls." She slapped the basket lid shut
and inclined her head. Kim and Kate scrambled down,
stopping before Nash. He squatted to meet their gaze
and gave each of them a quick kiss.

"What have you been doing all morning?" he asked.

"Laundry," they said, smiling.

"You never liked doing it with me."

"But with Miss Hayley—" the girls looked at her
adoringly "—it's fun."

"Well, we still have a ton of chores before party
time, ladies." She hooked a thumb toward the house
and the girls skipped on ahead.

Nash straightened, the motion bringing him inches
from her. He caught the scent of jasmine again, felt the
heat of her body. He took a step back. "Party time?"

"I've promised them a game or two. Is it all right if
they go in the pool?" At his hesitation, she added, "I'm
an excellent swimmer."

He knew that and hated to deprive the girls. "Sure, just let me know before you get in so I can check the chlorine."

"I already did." She turned away, not seeing his brows shoot up.

"Thanks, Miss Hayley," the men chimed.

"You're welcome, guys. Don't work too hard." She walked toward the house.

"Yeah, thanks," came a deep drawl, and Hayley sent a look over her shoulder.

"No sweat, boss. Just doing my job."

She wasn't. She didn't have to take the time to make the hands a midafternoon snack and certainly not bring it out here to them. They'd all had a decent lunch at noon. And Nash knew there was more than one person's share of work to get done in the house. He didn't like her calling him boss, either, then decided it would certainly remind him of the boundary between them.

Regardless of his thoughts, Nash watched her round behind shifting inside her short skirt, then dragged his gaze to his daughters. A little tinge of jealousy worked beneath his skin when the girls raced back to help her carry the basket.

"Sure was nice of her," Beau said, and Nash glanced at him. Great. The kid had a crush on her already.

Yet in the back of his mind a little voice whispered that she was going into the pool and that meant a bathing suit. Nash turned away, swinging onto his horse and riding down to the south fence. He'd be there for a couple of hours making repairs, he told himself. Anything to keep from seeing Hayley, half-naked, in a swimsuit.

Because then he'd remember what it was like to make love to her.

Two

Strike three.

She could cook.

Nash stood in his formal dining room and stared at the spread on the table. He wasn't sure what it was that smelled so good, yet the minute he'd entered the house, his mouth had started watering. The Hayley he'd known before couldn't boil water and had eaten food that came out of a can or could be nuked in a microwave. Unless he'd taken her out.

It was another reminder that she wasn't the same woman.

Behind him the ranch hands filed in, washed and shirts changed. His daughters were already sitting at their places near his, their plates prepared, beside them tall glasses of chocolate milk. He'd have to remind Hayley he preferred they didn't overdo it with the sugar.

"Have a seat, gentleman. Dinner is served."

Nash turned as she entered the area from the kitchen with a huge platter stacked with breaded chicken. The men scrambled for their seats as Nash slipped into his.

"I know your mamas taught you better, or am I going to have to hold this food hostage for y'all to take off those hats?" she said, eyeing them all except hatless Nash and Seth. Caps and cowboy hats disappeared under the table, and smiling with approval, she held the platter so they could serve themselves.

"What is it, Miss Hayley?" Beau asked, giving the platter a speculative look before stabbing a portion.

"Chicken Castellana. It's a recipe from an old friend's Sicilian nana. See, her husband, Angelo, was a barber, and during the depression people didn't have cash, so they paid him in day-old bread, chickens, potatoes, whatever." She shrugged, talking as she moved from man to man. "People had to have a haircut to get a job." Her glance slid meaningfully to Ronnie and he smirked. "Anyway, Nana Josie created this recipe from the payments. It's been cooking all afternoon."

She stopped beside Nash and bent to offer him the platter. He served himself, avoiding looking into those eyes.

"Don't be shy, Nash. There's plenty more still in the oven."

She was so close Nash felt the whisper of her breath skate down the side of his throat. He turned his head slightly and met her gaze. Her lips curved as if she knew her effect on him, and he focused on the platter, adding another piece to his plate. "Happy?"

"Ecstatic," she said, then set the platter down. "The gravy is there, and help yourselves to seconds." She went to the hutch, picking up the water pitcher and refilling the glasses before stopping beside the girls, bending to their level. "You two doing okay?"

They nodded vigorously, their mouths full. "Vegetables, too," Hayley said. They made faces, then after a glance at their dad, nodded. She tipped her head to Nash. "How is it?"

"Incredible." He didn't look up.

"Sorta ticked you off, huh?"

Now he did look at her. He stared, dumbfounded for a second as he chewed.

"Admit it. You didn't think I could handle it."

He swallowed. "I admit to nothing."

"Careful, Nash, your testosterone is dripping." His gaze narrowed and she blinked sweetly, then straightened, accepting compliments as she left the room.

Nash gazed down the length of the table, realizing there was no place setting for her. He left his chair and went into the kitchen. She was seated at the worktable on a high stool, her face in a medical book as she ate. She looked like a pixie figurine, her head bowed, the fork poised. The lonely picture made his heart drop, and forced him to see how little family she'd had in her life. How many times had she dined alone? Spent a holiday alone?

"Hayley."

She looked up.

"Aren't you joining us?"

She gave him a patient smile. "I'm the hired help, not a regular one at that." She'd done this kind of work enough to know it just wasn't wise to include herself at the dinner table.

"I'm sure the girls would like it."

"But I wouldn't."

His brows drew down and he stepped closer.

Her heart immediately picked up its pace. "I'm temporary, Nash. I don't want to give the girls any ideas just because you and I knew each other once."

"*Know* each other," he corrected, his eyes speaking volumes.

In the biblical sense, the long nights they'd spent exploring each other. It was hard to erase those images and even harder right now to remember the heartache she'd suffered. Especially when he looked at her the way he was now. With heat and memory.

She put the fork down, shaking her head. "Don't go there, please."

He moved closer, his broad-shouldered presence blocking out the light. "Hayley."

"No, Nash." She tipped her head back and met his gaze.

The sheen in her sable eyes knocked the breath from his lungs.

"I can't look at you across a dinner table without remembering that you walked away from me without a word." Her voice lowered to a heart-wrenching whisper. "Without remembering what it was like to be loved by you." Her lower lip quivered.

Nash felt sliced to ribbons. "Hayley. I need to tell—"

"No. You don't. Michelle told me all I needed."

His eyes darkened with suppressed anger. "I can just imagine."

"It doesn't matter. I'm a stone's throw away from my residency."

He straightened. "And like before, nothing is going to stop you."

She reared back a bit. "Can you blame me? I've worked hard for my degree."

"I know you have. But we both can see there's still something here between us."

"We can't relive the past. Too much has gone on."

"I know I've hurt you—"

She laughed, a short bitter sound. "Don't assume to know how I feel, Nash. As I recall, you never bothered to ask that seven years ago." He started to speak and she put up her hand. "It makes no difference to me now."

Nash ground his teeth. It did matter. Even if she was too stubborn to admit it. His daughters' and the ranch hands' voices filtered to the kitchen. This was not the place or the time to discuss this. But they would, dammit. They would. *And are you prepared to tell her the truth?* a voice pestered.

"Spend the time with your children, Nash. Ask how long they treaded water." She focused on the book and again Nash felt dismissed in his own house. He turned to the doorway. "And they helped make supper, too," she added.

That was a hint to praise them, and Nash felt like a heel for leaving the girls all the time. But that couldn't be helped and was the singular reason Hayley was here. He stepped back into the dining room.

Hayley bowed her head, clutching the book to her chest and swallowing the tears threatening to erupt. She thought she'd dealt with this years ago. Hadn't she gone on with her life? Hadn't she focused ever bit of energy on her education? Yet she was here, in his house, working for him and she hated it. Hated the reminders that said she'd never let him out of her heart. Oh, Lord. How could she ever forgive him when it hurt so badly just to see what she'd lost? The worst of it was that she'd loved him back then very deeply, and when he'd asked her to put her education on hold, to marry him and raise a family, she'd almost conceded. They'd fought over it. He just couldn't understand that she'd dreamed of being a doctor since she was a child. She couldn't let anything stop her then, and he was unwilling to compromise. Besides, she didn't know a thing about having a home and family. She'd had little of that herself. She'd wanted her career and knew if she'd given in to him, she'd never have gone back to school, and she would have resented him for it.

However, she never expected him to go straight into Michelle's arms.

Michelle had had her sights on Nash the instant he and Hayley had started dating. Hayley had known that, but she'd just never believed her own sorority sister would betray her or that Nash would fall for Michelle's helpless-Southern-belle bit. But that was only part of it. Hayley wasn't good enough for him. She didn't have the social graces, the impeccable background that Michelle Criswell had. Michelle was a socialite; she traveled in Nash's social circles, possessing all the proper qualities a man like Nash needed in a wife. Hayley, on the other hand, was nearly poverty-stricken, on scholarships and working two jobs to survive. She could never measure up to the Rayburn two-hundred-year-old lineage.

Michelle had flashed her indecently large engagement ring in her face and victoriously said just that.

Hayley sniffled and swallowed, reaching for a napkin to dry her tears. Then, she couldn't have made plans till she had her MD, and she couldn't now.

Nash's deep voice rumbled through the distance to the kitchen, making her heart skip and she looked up at

the wall separating the kitchen and dining room. *It's too
late to go back,* she thought.

"Calm down, Hayley."

"Calm down?" she said into the phone. "I swear,
Kat, if I was there, I'd—"

"Beat me senseless about the head and shoulders?"

Hayley's lips curved in a smile and she sighed.
"Yeah. But that would ruin your hairdo." She sank
onto the bed, rubbing her forehead. "How could you
do this to me?"

"Sugah, it was fate, I swear it. He called and you
were next on the list, available."

"Didn't you consider the position you put me in?"

"You can handle him. You're a strong woman, Hayley."

"And his former lover."

"It would have been rude to mention that."

"He doesn't want me here."

"How do you know that?"

Hayley scoffed. "I'm a bad penny turning up, Kat,
and the fact that I'm inches from residency is just one
reminder of why we split."

"And Michelle didn't have a thing to do with it,
right?"

Hayley didn't want to talk about Michelle. She was
dead, part of the past, unchangeable. No one, not even
Kat, knew the details of Nash's marriage. It was as if
he'd shut out the world then. And it was too painful a
subject to approach, especially with Nash. "Michelle
didn't tackle him till he and I argued. Besides, she had
all the right qualities, obviously, and—"

"That's bunk."

"—it wouldn't have worked," Hayley said as if Kat

hadn't spoken. "He wanted a wife and mother. I wanted a career. I still want that. Besides, I don't have time."

"You have two weeks."

Hayley didn't bother to comment on that.

"Fine, be that way." Kat paused and then said, "So, how's he look?"

Smiling at the purely feminine interest in Kat's voice, Hayley shook her head and flopped back onto the pillows. "Well, you know how fine wine gets with age."

"Oh, lawd, he must be devastating."

"An understatement." Wealthy, commanding, handsome, strong-willed and, as she recalled, a great kisser. What more could a girl ask for?

Kat's voice broke back into her thoughts. "His daughters?"

She smiled. "Beautiful. Sweet, well behaved."

"You're falling in love with them."

"Anyone with a heart would."

"And their daddy?"

"That is a dead subject, Kat. But..."

Kat jumped on her hesitation. "But what?"

"Nothing...it's nothing."

"Dag-gummit, Hayley Ann!"

Hayley smiled. *Let her stew,* she thought. *Kat deserves to be left out in the cold.* Not that there was anything to tell. "You know, Katherine, what goes around comes around."

"Hah! I wish something long-legged and slow talkin' like Nashville Rayburn would come calling around me."

Nashville. She'd forgotten about that little secret. "Careful what you wish for, you tart."

"Pest. Always were. Worst little sister I've ever sponsored." The love in Kat's tone was unmistakable.

Hayley heard voices, and frowning, she walked to her bedroom door and opened it, peering into the hall. It was coming from the girls' quarters upstairs. "I've got to go. I can hear Nash hollering, and he sounds like he's going to bust a vein or something."

"Well, you just go to him, then, sugah."

Distracted, Hayley didn't recognize the smugness in Katherine's voice before she cut the line and tossed the phone on the bed.

Had she, she might not have gone upstairs.

"Kimberly Grace Rayburn, open this door!"

"I can't, Daddy!"

"I promised not to come in, but you promised not to lock the door."

"We're fine, Daddy. We're not babies."

"But you're *my* babies." They just giggled. "I can get it open, you know."

"No!" the twins wailed.

Nash sighed, falling back against the wall and rubbing his hand over his face. They'd been at this for ten minutes and he didn't want them bathing without supervision. Why were they so shy around him lately?

"It's normal."

He opened his eyes to find Hayley standing nearby, a stack of towels in her arms. "I'm their father," he said.

"You're a male to them right now and they don't want you to see them naked."

"But I've seen them every day for five years!" He made a frustrated sound, then said, "They could drown!"

Hayley stepped close, knocking softly. "Hey, girls, can I come in?"

There was a bit of discussion in there and Hayley offered Nash a weak smile. Then the door lock clicked. Nash scowled. Hayley stepped inside. Nash started to move in, too, but Hayley waved him back, leaving the door open a discreet crack.

"What, no bubbles?"

"Bubbles?" The twins looked at each other and smiled. "Mrs. Winslow never let us have bubbles. She makes us hurry."

Nash scowled at that and he leaned against the wall, out of sight.

"Well," Hayley said, settling to the floor and taking up the washcloth and soap, "sometimes it's necessary, but a lady needs to soak in a bathtub of bubbles once in a while. It's a luxury *we* are allowed."

"Why?" Nash said from the hall.

"Because we are females, Nash. It's that time when we paint our toenails, ponder world affairs, pretty gowns, handsome men—" she winked at the girls, shampooing their hair "—soothe broken hearts and plan our futures."

"Broken hearts" clung to his mind and his throat tightened. Her voice was soft, her Southern accent refined and cultured, like his mom's. "I don't see the point of it," he said. "Get in, get out. Turning into a prune is a waste of time."

Hayley rolled her eyes and the girls copied her. "That's why you are a man and we are women. You will never understand."

"A girl thing," he said.

"Yes. Okay, ladies, time to rinse."

This was the hard part, Nash thought. Kate was scared to death of getting soap in her eyes. The water ran, but he didn't hear the usual complaints, and he peeked inside the room. Kate had a washcloth pressed tightly over her eyes and Hayley was doing her best to keep it from getting wet. Well, heck, he did that all the time, but got nothing but screams. When Kate was done, Hayley wrapped her head in a towel, then focused on Kim. Nash darted back when they stepped from the tub.

A few minutes later Kate said, "Okay, Daddy, you can come in now."

Nudging the door open, he swung around the door frame and smiled. "I knew my babies were under all that dirt." He kissed each twin, then reached for the comb. Kim winced before he even started.

Standing behind Kate, Hayley cleared her throat. He looked. She worked through the tangles in record time and Nash copied her moves, starting from the bottom in small increments. Kim twisted, looking at him and smiling. While they blow-dried pounds of hair, Nash's gaze kept slipping to Hayley's reflection in the mirror. She looked like the wild redhead he'd fallen in love with, and he'd never allowed himself to imagine her like this, with his daughters. He didn't want to consider how good it felt to have her here. She wasn't staying.

"You both have such beautiful hair," Hayley said, stroking the brush through Kate's long curls. Nash smiled at Kate's contented expression. She was almost purring.

The girls thanked her politely. "Daddy thinks we should get it cut."

Her gaze slid to Nash's. "That might not be such a bad idea, just for the summer. It is hot." His shoulders drooped a little and Hayley could tell he was relieved by the suggestion. "Think about it. We can look at magazines for a cut you'd like.'' The girls weren't receptive.

"Bedtime," Nash said.

The girls headed to their room, which was most of the upper floor, while Hayley gathered the wet towels.

"Thanks, Hayley."

She straightened, smiling.

"I would have spent half the night trying to get that bath done, with twice as much mess and a bucket of tears. I'm grateful."

Warmth spread through her. "No problem."

"I've been going through girl-panic like that for a week now."

"Just respect their privacy. Believe me, this is just the start of it." He groaned, reaching to help clean up, but she stayed his hand. "I have it. Go to your daughters."

He nodded, then walked into the bedroom and settled the girls into bed. He was at a disadvantage, just being male, and he realized how much his daughters enjoyed a younger more sympathetic female than Mrs. Winslow in the house. Mrs. Winslow was always ready to go home about this time of night, he recalled, and now he wondered if she was really ill or just tired.

Hayley stepped into the bedroom half an hour later and found Nash asleep in the chair between the twin beds, a storybook on his chest and his hands clasped around each of his daughters'. The tender scene stabbed through her with a longing so keen her breath snagged in her chest. Oh, to be loved and needed like this, she thought. To have a home and family. Nash was trying hard to be both father and mother and make a living at the same time, and she thought of how hard it must have been for her own father, raising her alone. She glanced around the room, just now noticing that, while there were several framed photos of Nash and the girls and other relatives, there were none of Michelle. None anywhere else in the house, either. Nor had the girls mentioned her. Not once. But then, Hayley thought, she rarely spoke of her own mother, her memories too faint to recall. Kim and Kate probably had no recollection of their mother. Since Michelle had died when they were infants, they'd never known her and really had no concept of her. Was that why there were no pictures?

Hayley moved to Nash, tapping him lightly on the shoulder. He stirred.

"You're going to regret it in the morning if you sleep in that chair all night," she whispered close to his ear.

His lips curved softly, his eyes still closed. "You still have the sweetest voice, Hayley."

"Say that when I get hopping mad."

His forehead wrinkled for a second. He'd never seen her mad. Not even hurt, really. He'd never given her the chance. He opened his eyes. Hayley was covering up his children, tucking their stuffed toys close. Her hand lingered over Kim's hair, and his throat tightened at the sight. Her expression was incredibly tender, and Nash thought of how easily Hayley gave, as if she'd known his girls for years.

He looked at his babies. How could their mother have walked away without a backward glance? The memory tormented him at times like this, when he knew his girls were missing a mother. He reminded himself that Hayley was temporary. And he didn't want his daughters to get so attached to her they'd be hurt when she left. But with Hayley, he thought, as she whispered good-night

and swept past him, well, it was just plain hard to keep
"temporary" in his mind.

Nash stayed in his office most of the next day, working on bids for the coming auction. The house was sur-
prisingly quiet, and though he made progress in his
work, the lack of activity and his curiosity forced him
out. The house was immaculate, and something heavenly simmered on the stove. He sampled a taste of the
stew, nearly burning his tongue. He called out. No answer. And he realized just how big this house was when
he was alone. A rare occurrence, he knew. Grabbing his
hat and striding to the front door, he flung it open and
stepped onto the porch. He spied Hayley out by her car,
then trotted down the steps and crossed the driveway.

With his daughters playing close by, she was bent
under the open hood of her car, grease on one bare
thigh.

Nash peered under the hood. "Good Lord, is that a
pair of panty hose for a fan belt?"

She jerked upright, knocking her head into his chin.
"Ow, yes, it is." She rubbed her head. "A girl has to
make do when she's alone on a dark country road."

"All the more reason to get a better car. This thing
is falling apart."

"Not quite yet." She leaned back under the hood to
adjust the panty-hose belt. "Besides, Lurlene just needs
a rest, dontcha, baby?" She patted the fender. "Can you
hand me the torque wrench?" She waved at the toolbox
behind her. He pushed the wrench into her hand.

"Why are you fixing this now?" he asked when she
straightened.

"The girls and I are going to the market to pick up
some household stuff."

His features tightened. "You're not taking my children anywhere in that pile of junk!"

"Shh." She covered up a headlight as if covering ears. "Insults won't make Lurlene your friend, Nash."

His lips twitched. Hayley always did have a great sense of humor.

"So what do you propose I do?" she asked.

He folded his arms over his chest and called for Jimmy Lee. The ranch hand came around the corner of the barn, hopped the fence and strode toward them.

"Yeah, boss?"

"Bring the sedan around for Miss Albright, will you?"

"Sedan?" Hayley said, looking for one in the yard. There were half a dozen trucks, flatbeds, and five horse trailers neatly lined up behind the breeding barn, but no sedan.

"Want me to drive her?" Jimmy asked.

Nash glared. The man was eyeballing Hayley's bare legs and cropped T-shirt as if she were spicy barbecue on a summer night. "No, I do not. She's capable of driving herself and the twins."

"You trust me with the girls?" Hayley asked.

He met her gaze. "Of course," he said as if she was foolish to ask.

She smiled, a bright burst of light in dimples and dark-brown eyes. It hit him like a punch to the gut and rocked him to his boot heels. He could get used to seeing that every day, he thought as she took off like a shot, as usual, to the house to change her clothes. Someone ought to tie her down. But he was afraid if someone did, her impatient energy would drill a hole straight to China.

Two hours later Hayley drove back up the long gravel lane in his sedan. A Mercedes sedan, she thought, running her hand over the leather-covered steering wheel. The corporate car, he'd called it. It looked as if it had never been used. Even smelled new—and expensive. But then, he could afford to be extravagant. Before she and the twins had left, he'd told her to charge all she needed on his credit line, and anyone else might have been tempted to go hog-wild. But Hayley had pinched pennies for too long to go loose now.

She frowned when she pulled into the spot nearest the house and realized her car was missing. Climbing out, she shooed the girls inside and went to the trunk for the groceries. She had two sacks in her arms when Nash, on a beautiful chestnut stallion, rode down from the hill. He stopped on the edge of the driveway, and she tried not to notice how sexy he looked.

"Where's my car?" she asked.

"I had it towed."

Her gaze narrowed and she cocked her head. "Excuse me?"

"It's a piece of junk and dangerous, Hayley."

"And it's my piece of junk, not yours."

"If you're worried about your things, I had them delivered to your room."

How good of His Lordship, she thought. "It's *my* car, Nash."

His brow knitted. "Lurlene is held together with tape, panty hose and gum, darlin'. Give her a decent burial and get another."

"If I could afford one, don't you think I would be driving it?"

"I'll buy you one, then."

Instantly she dumped the bags back in the trunk.

"Get down off that horse so I can yell at you right proper." She pointed to the ground in case he misunderstood.

Smothering a smile, he swung down, tugging the fingers of his gloves as he walked closer.

She was in his face. "I don't need your charity, Nash Rayburn. And I resent the hell out of you taking charge of my car."

"If you want it back, I'll just make a call."

Her anger withered a bit. "Yes, I do. You do that. Right now."

He nudged his hat back. "I was only trying to help."

"You were manipulating. Doing what you damn well please because you have the money. Here's a novel approach," she said, wide-eyed and sarcastic. "How about asking me how I feel?"

"You would have said no."

"But you went ahead, pretty as you please."

"I can't have you driving that thing."

His superior look made her want to kick him. "Why? An embarrassment to you?"

"No, dammit, you could get hurt."

She held his gaze steadily, yet her voice wavered. "Any more than I already have been shouldn't matter to you, Nash."

She turned away and grabbed the grocery bags, sidestepping out of his reach when he tried to help.

"Hayley!"

"Don't talk to me till Lurlene is sitting next your stuck-up sedan!"

She didn't talk to him. She wouldn't even acknowledge him at dinner until the tow truck pulled away. And then she just gave him a "Don't try that again or you'll be sorry'' glare and headed into the house, his five-year-old traitors tucked by her side.

He looked at the rusted blue two-door coupe. Then he kicked it. The bumper fell off the back.

"I saw that!" came a voice from the house, and Nash had to smile. Having Hayley Albright around certainly made life interesting. Again.

Three

He'd been fine.

Just damn fine, controlling his desire for her, avoiding her when he wanted to touch her so badly. Until he'd walked around the back of the house, purely by chance to look for his misplaced pocket knife, and saw her naked.

Well, almost naked.

Bare-chested, Nash slammed the ax into the wood, its splintering crack vibrating over the hillside.

She might as well have been naked for all the skin that bathing suit hid.

He kept his back to the house and put another log on the stump, bringing the ax down again. Then another and another, until the waistband of his jeans was drenched with sweat. It didn't do a damn thing for the unsatisfied desire running heavily through his blood.

He split another log, then threw down the ax, and

stacked the wood for curing till winter. He didn't look
toward the house or the pool deck. Because she was
there. In a hot pink bikini. Tonga style. He closed his
eyes and briefly shook his head. He was in real danger
and hoped the ranch hands didn't get a look at all that
flesh.

She'd cause a stampede.

He added another split log to the seven-foot-high
stack, then swept up the ax again. The blow sent two
halves flying outward.

"Hi."

Head bowed, Nash propped the ax head on the stump,
his wrist on the handle top. He didn't turn around. "Hi
yourself."

"Aren't you even going to look at me?" Hayley
asked.

"You still wearing that scrap of nothing you call a
swimsuit?"

"Yes, I am." He heard a light laugh. "Nash. This is
silly."

He flipped the ax up and placed another log on the
stump. He split it and even without looking, he felt her
flinch.

"What did I do?"

"Nothing."

"Nash." He could hear the hurt in her voice. "If this
is about the car—"

"Go on back to the girls," he interrupted.

"Gladly, boss. Enjoy your own company."

Nash cursed under his breath. It wasn't the stupid car.
It was her! Seeing her, wanting her, even arguing with
her slammed desire and regret through him. The guilt
over what he'd done, what honor and duty had pushed
him to do at her expense made him angry. With himself.

He didn't deserve her kindness. He didn't deserve her thoughtful gestures or her concern. Or anything else for that matter. And that he couldn't alleviate his guilt in telling the truth was a burden that wore on him the longer she was near. He wanted to, but his sins were just too ugly. She'd never forgive him, anyway, he thought, and wished the two weeks were over and she was gone. And at the same time he prayed they'd never end. *Wish in one hand and spit in the other and see what you get,* he thought.

He glanced over his shoulder. She was walking down the hillside toward the pool where his daughters were having a snack in the shade of the stone veranda. He absorbed everything about her as she moved, noticing not only that she wore a cover-up over that too-hot-to-be-legal bikini, but that her head was bowed and she hugged herself.

He felt like a first-class heel. Then his gaze fell on another splitting stump a few feet away. A pitcher of ice water sparkled in the hot sun, beside it a glass and wrapped sandwich, a little plastic horse on a toothpick stuck in the center.

Nash groaned.

Something had to be done. Soon.

Or he was going to go just plain nuts.

Nash rushed the horse, trying to get the animal to obey his commands, but it wasn't going well. He attributed that to his wandering mind, and that irritated him to no end. He hadn't seen Hayley since breakfast, and that had been a little strained, especially after his unfounded harshness the day before. Last night after the girls went to bed, she'd disappeared into her room, and he hadn't bothered her, afraid that whatever he said would just stamp "You're so hot, I can't even think straight" across his forehead. She made him too aware of the fact that he was a man and she was a beautiful woman.

And how good it had once been between them.

And how he'd blown it.

He heard giggles and glanced up, catching a glimpse of Hayley and his daughters heading for the chicken coop. She was wearing jeans, boots and a lime-green T-shirt, like his girls, and he thought how cute the three of them looked. Hayley's red hair gleamed in the sunlight.

"They sure do like her," Seth said from a few feet away.

"Yeah," Nash said, not taking his eyes off the trio.

"Want me to go see if they need help?"

"She'll come for it if she needs it." One thing he remembered about Hayley was that she could do just about anything she set her mind to.

Nash turned to the horse, swinging up onto the bare back. The wild thing bucked, sending his hat to the ground, yet he held on, riding out the mare's temper. Slipping off, he led the horse around the ring, his daughters' laughter breaking through his concentration. He glanced and waved before his gaze swung to Hayley. She looked worried. He scooped up his hat and turned back to the horse, trying to ignore her. But his gaze kept straying to her as the girls showed her how to spread a little grain on the ground, then fill the troughs for the chicken and pigs. They collected eggs and he could see Hayley's sour expression from here. He smirked. Well, at least she'll get a taste of real ranching, he thought, then remembered how Michelle had protested against going within twenty feet of the coop. He should have seen that coming, recognized her true distaste for ranching. Or was it just him? Irritated with his train of thought, especially when he could scarcely drag Michelle's image from the waste of his mind, he led the horse into the barn. He'd just handed over the currying to Jimmy when he heard his daughters scream.

"Daddy! Come quick!"

Racing out of the barn, Nash bolted to the pigpens and found his daughters safe beyond the fence, but Hayley was in the sty, on her rear. He leaped the rail and hurried through the mire. She tried to stand, but the pigs were crowding her, snorting over her hair and face, leaving a black muddy trail.

"Be still!" Nash yelled. But she wasn't. She scrambled to her knees, then fell back down.

"We haven't been properly introduced, but I think they like me," she joked, yet he heard her fear. Nash yelled and shoved at the pigs. The pigs lumbered off as he scooped her up in his arms, slung her over his shoulder and made his way out of the pens.

"This isn't necessary. I'm capable of—"

"Hush, woman." Unceremoniously he set her on her feet.

She staggered back a step. "Thank you, I—"

"What in Sam Hill possessed you to get in there?"

She blinked up at him. "I dropped the bucket and was trying to fetch it."

His gaze swung to his daughters. "You two didn't tell her that you are never to go in there?"

The twins stepped back a little, not saying a word.

"Nash—"

He looked at Hayley. "No." His hand sliced the air.

"They know better and it's their responsibility to tell you the rules."

"It was my fault. I didn't even consider the danger."

"About ten of those animals are wild boar! Didn't you see the tusks?" He pointed to the pen. "You could have been trampled and gored. You're just a little thing and obviously know nothing about pigs and how mad they can get!"

She stepped closer, flinging mud off her arms. "So what are you upset about? That you had to stop work long enough to rescue me? That I could have been hurt and not be able to work? That I made a mistake?" She drew in a deep breath, her hands on her hips. "Or do you just need an excuse to yell at me?"

"I'm not yelling!"

Laughter prickled the air.

Nash's gaze snapped to the three ranch hands leaning over the corral fence, entertained by the scene. His glare sent them back to work. He looked back at Hayley. She was covered with mud. His daughters were behind her like little stone guards.

"Let's not talk about danger when you rode that wild horse!" She was in his face. "And at your age."

"My age? I've been doing this all my life!"

"Well, I've been doing this for about four days now, Nashville, so I think you should give me a break!" She spun around, grabbing the egg basket and corralling the girls before the threesome marched to the house.

Nash tore off his hat and slammed it to the ground, his breathing heavy. Damn fool woman! She could have been killed! He paced for a few minutes, trying to get control of his heartbeat, then headed to the house.

"Don't you dare track mud in here, Nash Rayburn,"

he heard her shout the instant he stepped across the threshold. "I just washed that floor!"

He froze. "Then come here!"

"No. Go back to work. I'm fine."

The girls peered around the corner of the foyer wall.

"Where is she, Kim?" Hesitantly Kim looked at her sister, then her dad.

"In the bathroom," Kate said. "Cleaning up."

Nash toed off his boots, rolled up his muddy pant legs, then strode past his daughters, who flattened against the wall. He stopped at the bathroom. The door was half-open and Hayley stood there in lime-green bra and panties, bent over the sink, washing the dirt from her arms, face and hair. She was a head full of lather and a body full of delectable bare skin. Every hormone he owned jumped up and shouted, and he was helplessly transfixed as she rinsed, reached for a towel and straightened.

She gasped, covering herself with the towel. "Boy, you've got your nerve." She started to close the door on him.

His hand kept it open. Water dripped off her hair, making rivers over her shoulders to the swells of her breasts.

"Quit looking at me like that, Nash, 'cause I don't like you very much right now."

His gaze snapped to hers and he tried keeping it there. "That was careless."

Her expression fused with fresh anger. "You overreacted." She grabbed her robe off a hook and turned her back, pulling it on. Then she rounded on him. "You didn't have to upbraid me in public, and the girls are too young to remember rules like that." She yanked the sash tight. "They'll bow to an adult's decision most any time.'' She was in his face again, poking his chest. ''And *you* should have told me the rules.''

''I see that now.'' His gaze locked with hers, Nash knew he could get used to being this close to her, feeling her temper, then the fizzle of it. ''I apologize.''

''Accepted.''

He frowned. ''That sure as hell doesn't sound like it.''

''That's your problem. The matter is over.''

Nash stared into her eyes and knew she was saying more than that. And he didn't like it.

''Why did you get so mad, Daddy?''

Nash twisted around. His daughters were staring up at him, on the verge of tears. He felt like a creep and knelt to face them. ''I was scared.''

''Why?'' Kim asked, and he knew from experience that a series of logical questions needed to be answered before the girls were satisfied.

''Because I thought the hogs would crush Miss Hayley.''

Clearly this was not enough explanation for his daughters. ''But you yelled.''

''That happens sometimes when a person...'' He searched for words they'd understand.

''Blames themselves for the danger being there in the first place,'' Hayley finished for him, and Nash swung his gaze up to hers.

''Yeah,'' he conceded.

''I'm not glass, you know.''

She was. She was small and frail, and if he'd thought earlier she could handle ranch life, this just proved him wrong. ''Ask Seth about getting stomped by a wild pig. They weigh about 350 pounds.''

She was shocked. But she'd never been on a ranch

before, nor near so much livestock. There was a lot to learn. Not that she'd be around long enough to learn it. "Then the girls shouldn't be near them, either."

He eyed her.

She arched a brow. "Your gates, the pen—they're pig-stampede-proof, then? You can guarantee it?"

He shook his head, not liking that she'd pointed out something he should have seen before now.

Kim said, "I'm sorry, Daddy."

He looked at the twins. "No, Daddy's sorry, baby. It's not your fault." Although he was covered in mud, he hugged them. "We'll all be extra careful next time."

"We promise," they chimed.

"Go on and get some juice," Hayley said, leaning around Nash. "I'll be along and we can finish the chores." They girls glanced between the adults, then left.

"I want you to go over the details with me ASAP," she said to him. "I think you scared them."

"I know I did."

He looked worried about it and her anger waned. "Go on back to work, Nash. I'll smooth things over." He eyed her. "I'll make you look like a gallant knight, trust me."

Somehow he doubted that now. "Don't go overboard. I have trouble living up to their ideals as it is." He gave her a towel. "You're still dripping." Water sparkled on her hair. He stepped closer, the heat of his body penetrating the thin terry-cloth robe.

She didn't move a muscle. "Don't even think about it."

He smiled tenderly, liking the breathy apprehension in her voice. "Think about what?"

Oh, he did not do "innocent" well, she thought. "Kissing me."

"I wasn't."

"You lie like a rug."

"I was thinking about doing a hell of a lot more than kissing." He bent, tucking a finger under her chin and tipping up her face. His mouth was a fraction from hers. "I'm just apologizing like any real gentleman."

Delicious tremors swept through her, making her insides heavy with want. "I already accepted it."

"Not enough." His breath scattered across her lips.

Hayley was tempted—boy was she tempted—but self-preservation and old hurt won out. She pressed a hand to his lips, halting him. His gaze swept to hers.

"Don't. This will lead nowhere except heartache." She was surprised she managed to get the words past her lips with him looking at her like that. "And I've been there."

Nash realized the magnitude of what he was doing and eased back. Hadn't he spent the better part of the day chopping a cord of wood trying to avoid this? She didn't want to be part of his life. She'd made that clear before and she was doing it again now. A temporary wife. A doctor launching her new career. He should heed his own advice and be the wiser.

Nodding mutely, he stepped a few feet away before looking back at her. He thought he saw disappointment in her eyes just then, but he couldn't be sure.

At the soft rap on his office door, Nash muttered a response and kept entering data into the computer.

"Hey. Want some coffee or something stronger?"

His gaze flew to hers, then took in her damp hair and her pajamas and matching robe—dark brown with pink sheep jumping over fences. There was nothing revealing about the robe, yet all he could see was her delectable shape beneath.

Hayley felt it. He looked between the tray and her pajamas as if she were Mata Hari holding a magnum of champagne and about to seduce the secrets of the free world from him.

It thickened the air between them.

"Well?"

He blinked. "Sure."

"Which is it?" She held up a tray with a bottle and glass on one side and a carafe of coffee on the other.

"Coffee."

That figures, Hayley thought. Far be it for him to stop and relax. She never knew anyone who was so driven, yet ignorant of his surroundings, expecting everyone to toe the line as hard as he did. Granted, he had the most at risk. But even she knew when it was time to kick back and sit a spell.

Setting the tray down on the edge of his desk, careful not to disturb the papers, she poured him a cup, adding just a splash of cream.

Nash accepted it. It was just the right color. He sipped, feeling the tension in the room grow since she'd slipped through the door.

He tried for a safe subject. "Dinner was great, Hayley." He hadn't eaten this well since his mother had lived here.

"Thank you, sah," she drawled. "There was a little vengeance in serving a roasted pork loin."

He smiled into his cup. "So when did you become a culinary master?"

She scoffed. "Necessity. The need to eat and have money for school." Her smile faded a little. "It's taken me six years to do what most people do in four. I've had to work, save, go to school, then stop and work some more till I got the money for the next semester."

He wanted to offer her money to make it easier on her, but he knew she wouldn't accept it. "What else have you done?"

"You name it. I'm a jack-of-all-trades," she said, reaching over to freshen his coffee. She sent him a look asking his permission as she lifted the bottle of bourbon. He nodded and she poured a swallow into the glass. "Working for Wife Incorporated fits my schedule and the pay is good."

He relaxed back in his chair, watching as she strolled around the room, looking at trophies and framed belt buckles.

Hayley hadn't been in here before. As he'd said on the first day, it was off-limits and she'd respected that. She glanced around, wondering if the twins ever came in here. "This is your sister, Samantha, right?" She pointed to one photo among several on the wall. He nodded. "She's beautiful." Though they'd never had the chance to meet, Hayley recognized the resemblance in the dark hair, the piercing blue eyes. And the love in the eyes of the man standing next to her. Samantha was married to a man named Daniel, the girls had mentioned.

"Thanks, not that I had anything to do with it. She had every man for miles chasing her. Daniel caught her before my parents threatened to send her away."

"A little too wild?"

He scoffed, smiling to himself. "If my father knew everything she did, he'd have sent her away the minute she started—" He stopped.

She cocked an eyebrow at him. "Growing breasts?"

"Matured," he said. She grinned and he sipped coffee, then leaned over to splash some bourbon into the cup.

"Does your brother, Jake, live near?" She pointed to the photo of a younger version of Nash—dark hair, blue eyes and a captivating smile. He was standing with a prize-winning horse and wearing the biggest rodeo belt buckle she'd ever seen.

"Close. Next county."

Hayley felt his gaze follow her as she moved around the large room. The furniture was dark burgundy overstuffed leather, the coffee and end tables wrought-iron and glass. Terribly masculine and seductive, she thought. Even the shiny garnet walls and white crown molding lent an air of sensuality. Like the man, she thought, sparing him a glance. He was still watching her, his gaze sliding like silk and leaving steam behind. It wasn't fair that after all this time he could make her heart skip a beat with just a look, she thought, sipping the bourbon, feeling it warm her throat. She examined the Civil War relics on the mantel—a ball shot, the workings of a gun with small chunks of wood stock still there. Under glass in a shadow box was a pair of spectacles, a stick of graphite in a metal case like a mechanical pencil and a faded letter with its envelope.

She peered. "It's a love letter."

"From one of my ancestors to his wife." Nash left the chair and rounded the desk to stand beside her. "You can barely read the writing, but he mentions that they were headed to Pennsylvania." He caught a whiff of perfume and freshly washed hair. It made him ache.

She inhaled. "Gettysburg?"

"Yeah, he died there. This came home with his personal things and a letter from his commanding officer."

"Oh, that's heartbreaking." She covered her heart, her look romantically sympathetic. "He never got to send the letter."

"He left three children and a wife. Here in this house."

She blinked up at him. "It's *that* old?"

"Over 225, near as we can figure."

"Mercy." She looked around the room as if she could see above and outside. "It's amazing your family still has it."

"A Rayburn kept it during the revolution and the Civil War by lending horses to the army."

She met his gaze. "I admire that, Nash. Not many people can put a finger on their roots and say, this is where it began, where I come from." She scarcely remembered her grandfather, and even her mother's face was a faded image in her mind.

Nash looked down at the cup, the bourbon separating the coffee with its strength, and thought about how little she'd had in her life to comfort her. And when the opportunity was near, he'd snatched it away. It had been duty, he reminded himself. His honor had been at stake.

He drained the cup and crossed to his desk. He stared to pour more, then set the bottle down. The only thing that had saved him in the past years were his daughters. They'd needed him and he'd had to force himself to focus on their needs, instead of his own.

Until Hayley walked back into his life.

He watched her as she continued to move around the room. When she came to a small butler tucked in the corner, she froze. Nash felt it from across the room, the stillness in her, fragile, as if one touch would make her crumble to dust. His brows drew down as he moved to her. He stopped a few feet away. His gaze snapped to her, then slid to the photo on the butler.

It was a picture of his wedding day.

Hayley drained the rest of the bourbon, still staring. "She looks…lovely."

"On that day she was."

Hayley couldn't look at him. It hurt too much. "You say that as if it was the only time."

He scoffed and went to the desk, sloshing more liquor into the coffee mug. "She's dead. I'd rather not talk about it."

Hayley felt her throat close tight. "You loved her."

He stilled, the mug halfway to his mouth. "Don't ask, Hayley. Please."

The agony in his voice was clear enough. "I never understood."

He twisted to look at her. Her finger grazed the crystal frame. An invisible fist wrapped around his heart, squeezing the life from him. "Understood what?"

"Why you left me without a word and went to her."

"And you think you do now?"

Her nod was so miniscule he almost didn't catch it.

"You loved her," she said again.

The tears in her voice slayed him where he stood. He clenched his fists.

"You loved her and you used me."

"That's not true."

She snapped a look at him, venom in her bright eyes. "Then what is, Nash? I have a right to know after all this time how you could say you loved me and wanted me to give up my dreams for a life with you, then betray me!"

His features went taut with his own misery, and he rubbed his hand over his face.

"I never even got the chance to show you my anger. Do you know how humiliating it was to learn from Michelle I was tossed aside? Everyone knew we'd been together. Everyone." She shuddered with the force of holding back her tears. "You made me look like the campus tramp, good enough to take to bed, but not good enough to marry into the rich and powerful Rayburn family."

"Aw, Hayley, darlin', no, that's not it."

"It is! Your fiancée flashed an engagement ring in my face and in front of my sorority sisters and said I was just white trash and should have known the only thing I could get from you was crumbs." She bit her lip, years of anger and hurt and shame sweeping through her. "I can't do this. I can't stay here anymore." She rushed toward the door.

Panic seized him. "Hayley, no!"

She put up a hand, the other on the knob.

"She was pregnant."

She stopped and spun around, sucking in a great gulp of air. Her gaze searched his. "You bastard! You slept with her!"

Four

Her devastated expression carved a wound on his soul. Finally he nodded.

"While you were seeing *me?*"

He held her gaze and she read the truth.

If she could have crumbled even more, she did. Shame sluiced through him like hot oil, burning a hole deep into his heart.

Hayley immediately stormed across the room, stopping inches from him. Then she slapped his cheek. His head whipped to the side with the force, and he worked his jaw for a second before looking at her.

She made to slap him again and he snagged her wrists, wrestling with her until she crumbled in his arms.

She sobbed into his shirtfront, sorrow-filled cries as if her heart were shattering into a million pieces. "I loved you," she moaned, twisting out of his grasp and pounding his chest. "I loved you!"

"I know, honey, I know." He sighed wearily and wanted nothing more than to cradle her in his arms, but knew she wouldn't have it. "That night we argued about our future I thought I'd already lost you to your career. I went home and drank." He held her back enough to look her in the eye. "A little too much. Around midnight, Michelle was on my doorstep and throwing herself into my arms."

She shoved away. "I don't think I want to hear this."

He caught her elbow and spun around to face him. "Oh, yes, you will. You wanted to know the truth and you'll listen to all of it. About how I woke up the next morning and she was lying beside me, naked, and I didn't even remember letting her into the apartment. I don't even remember having sex with her."

She searched his eyes, wanting to believe him. "But you and I went to Jekyll Island the weekend after that fight, Nash." Her brows drew tight. They'd almost worked out their problems then. "So that's why you were so quiet."

Seeing the accusation in her eyes made his survival skills rear up. He had to make her understand, no matter what came later. "I couldn't tell you because I didn't remember it."

She wrenched off his touch as if it stained her clothes. "A man doesn't forget making love to a woman, Nash."

"He does when there's nothing to remember."

Her head was pounding with confusion. "But you said she was pregnant."

"*She* said she was. I had to believe her. Especially

when I calculated the weeks. So I did what I had to do.''

''You married her to give the children your name.''

''I made the mistake and I had to make it right. It was a matter of duty, Hayley.''

''What about your duty to me?'' she cried, angry again. ''And I might believe this pile of horse dung, Nash, if your daughters weren't a year too young for this story.'' Disgusted, she headed for the door. She'd leave tonight and head to Kat's in Savannah.

''That's because she lied.''

Hayley spun around, her breath lodged in her throat. ''Oh, you better talk fast, Rayburn.''

''She wasn't pregnant, but I didn't realize the truth till after the wedding. Weeks after.'' Nash pushed his fingers through his hair and held on to the back of his neck, feeling drained and alone. ''She played us both for fools. And after I learned that, she admitted we'd never had sex.'' He let his arms fall to his sides, re-membering his outrage, the hurt and, worse, knowing he'd abandoned Hayley for nothing. Nothing.

He met her gaze and for a moment, they stared in silence.

Nash kept his features impassive, waiting to see what she'd do; if she'd leave now and never look back, or if she'd stay and at least talk to him.

Crossing the room, Hayley sank into the sofa, her heart numb. Nash's shoulders slumped and he moved to the sideboard and poured her a small splash of bour-bon, adding some water. He started to move away, then stopped to fold the wedding picture facedown.

He went to her, holding the glass in her line of vision.

She tipped her head back. ''Pawns.''

Nash released a long slow breath. ''Yeah.''

She took the drink, but didn't taste it. "What did you do?"

He shrugged. "What could I do? I'd lost you and I was married. We were living closer to town then. She wanted to live here, but when my parents learned the truth, my mother didn't want her at River Willow."

"That must have been hard for you."

He dropped into a chair. How like Hayley to think of him at a time like this. "It was, but Michelle didn't seem to care. But when Dad died, we had to move in to help. After a while Mom decided she couldn't stand it and got a house about thirty miles from here."

"Michelle forced her out?"

Nash shook his head. "Michelle hardly spoke to her. But it was me Mom couldn't stand to look at."

Tapered brows rose. "Your own mother?"

"She knew I was unhappy." He held her gaze. "And she knew I'd loved you and what I'd done." Her features tightened and she looked down. Nash kept to himself that his mother had always been Hayley's champion, though they'd never met. Hayley didn't need to hear that right now, especially when he'd ignored his mother's advice and paid dearly.

"I tried to make the marriage work, but when the twins came along, Michelle couldn't handle them. She wasn't exactly prepared for the demands of motherhood on her social schedule." His lips twisted with bitterness. "She expected me to hire a nanny for the girls so she could go off playing rich man's wife. This is a working plantation, but she didn't feel it was necessary for her to work it. However, she liked the money. She was hoping I'd turn the work all over to Jake and go traveling around the world."

Hayley curled into the couch, pulling her feet up with

her. That certainly sounded like Michelle. "I guess I shouldn't complain, then."

Nash was slumped in the chair, his hands folded on his stomach. "You have every right to hate the Rayburns, Hayley. Me especially."

That just wasn't possible, but she didn't mention that. This was all too much to take in.

"The day of the accident, she'd packed her things, asked for a divorce, and when I said I would fight her for the girls, she said don't bother and walked out, abandoning me, her babies and this life she'd manipulated to get." The hurt in his eyes was like a bleeding wound.

"Thank God she didn't take the girls with her."

His gaze swung to hers. "Oh, I do. Every day."

"How could she walk away from her babies?" She shook her head. It was unthinkable to her. "The girls don't know a thing about this, do they?"

"No, just my mother. She got caught in the middle of it when we moved in after Dad died."

Hayley dipped her finger into the glass, then sucked the tip. Finally she looked up.

Nash's features pulled taut at the sorrow on her face.

"Why didn't you come tell me this, instead of letting me think the worst? You just stopped calling, stopped coming by, stopped everything."

He straightened in the chair. "I couldn't see you again. I loved you so much and I knew if I saw you or heard your voice, I wouldn't do the honorable thing. I had a duty to take care of my mistakes, Hayley. My family's reputation rode on it."

It was a quiet moment before she said very softly, "And if you had seen me?"

He rubbed his face again. "I would have run away with you to some deserted spot and never looked back."

Her throat burned. Tears filled her eyes and rolled slowly down her flushed cheeks. "Damn you for not coming to me," she said in a broken whisper. "Damn your Rayburn pride."

Nash listened to her suffering, to the quiet pain-filled sobs of a woman robbed of her heart's desire. He wanted so badly to take her in his arms and soothe her.

Then in a tiny voice she said, "I could have been their mother."

He nodded, his heart aching for her. "You should have been."

She stared at him. Regret shaped her features, reaching out to him, washing over him. He felt it, shared it, reliving the torment of having to give her up for a woman he didn't love.

His eyes burned and over the stone in his throat he whispered, "I...I'm so sorry, sprite."

She lowered her gaze, as if looking at him caused her more pain. Then she unfolded from the couch and crossed to the door. Nash frowned, following her as she walked down the hall. She went into her room, slipping silently into bed.

He stood in the doorway, his body a black shadow haloed in yellow light. "Hayley?"

"I can't talk about this anymore. It's too much."

He stepped into the room and pulled the quilt over her, kneeling beside the bed. Her eyes fluttered open, brown eyes bleary from tears, from the pain she'd suffered at the hands of people she'd trusted. "I'm sorry, baby. If I could change the past—"

She worked her hand out from under the quilt and laid two fingers over his lips. "It's done, Nash. Now we go on."

Nash took heart in that and leaned forward to press a kiss to her hair.

Hayley closed her eyes, absorbing the sensation of his touch. He left, closing the door behind him, and she prayed the bourbon did its job and let her sleep without dreams of everything that might have been.

The air was damp and breezy. Her skin simmered with sensual heat. His hands slid down her body, shaping her breasts, and he paused to suckle wetly on one tight pink tip, then continued his quest downward, his hand and lips and tongue leaving her writhing mindlessly with desire. Not an inch of her skin escaped his attention. He caressed her waist, her hips, smoothed his hands down her thighs and up the inside. Then he spread her, hovering over her pulsing body as he parted her flesh and stroked the fire to a raging inferno. She gasped, arching her body in a lover's call for more, to deepen his touch, then to fill her. He crawled up over her body, his thighs rasping against hers, then again he opened her for him, to plunge and—

Hayley sat up, gasping for air. She blinked in the darkened room, then threw off the covers and swung her legs over the side of the bed. Bending over, she cupped her face in her hands and took several deep breaths. The dream was so real. She could almost feel his hands on her, the hardness of him pressing into her. Her body screamed for him, unfulfilled desire throbbing through every pore. Perspiration clung and she stood, fluffing her pajama top, then shucking the bottoms. Despite the air-conditioning, her skin was hot and tingling. *This is so not fair,* she thought.

He hurts me and I still want him. She tried deciphering whether or not it was old feelings coming back or the hurt and the need to be soothed shadowing her dreams. It didn't make any difference, she thought tiredly. She couldn't consider starting up with him again, not in any shape or form. It just wouldn't be wise to fall back into a relationship when it had nowhere to go. She was leaving. For good. She had to do her residency. People were depending on her to be at the hospital.

Glancing at the clock, she realized she had to be up in half an hour, anyway, so going back to bed was not an option. Raking her fingers through her hair, she sighed gustily, then threw on some clothes. She left her room, heading to the kitchen for some ice water and maybe a clearer perspective before everyone else awoke.

Especially Nash.

Nash rolled onto his back and jammed a pillow under his head. He gave up on trying to sleep and stared at the drape of fabric flowing over the four poster bed. Last night he'd sat alone in the darkened study and nursed a drink he didn't want, thinking of the woman he couldn't have. Everything was out on the table before them. At least they had that. But she still hadn't forgiven him. He needed to hear the words. For seven years he'd held the guilt inside, done what was expected. So why didn't he feel free of it?

Because she'll never trust you again.

He was looking for trust when she might not forgive him. It would be just penance. Then a horrible thought occurred to him. What if she'd left in the middle of the night? Throwing back the covers, he pulled on his jeans before leaving his bedroom. He paused outside her door, then pushed it open. The bed was made and the room looked vacant.

The sight made his heart leap to his throat and stay there.

Then he heard the clang of pots and caught the scent of bacon. His relief was overwhelming and he strode quickly down the hall, crossing the foyer and padding on bare feet through the dining room to the kitchen. He saw her shuffling around the kitchen, preparing breakfast. She didn't look any better than he felt.

With a quick glance around, he realized they were alone. The girls would sleep late, but the ranch hands would be coming in for coffee in a few minutes. He watched her for a second, wondering what to say.

"It's impolite to stare, Nash."

"Then put more clothes on."

Hayley glanced down at her shorts and T-shirt, then lifted her gaze to his. "You need to address this problem you have with my clothes, and you shouldn't talk." He was wearing jeans, only jeans, and he looked so vulnerable standing in the doorway. But he wasn't. Even with the shadow of a beard and finger-combed hair, even with the hard-muscled chest shouting to be touched, he was still invincible to her.

Except the dark smudges under his eyes told her that while she'd slept, he hadn't.

She turned her gaze away, a dozen feelings running through her at once. She didn't think she could handle a single one right now. She'd spent the past hour trying to line them up in neat little rows only to have one look at his wary expression and experience the domino effect. Feelings fell all over themselves, confusing her more. She didn't want him to suffer any more than she had. He'd paid a higher price for that one night with

Michelle. And seeing people suffer and wanting to do something about it was why she'd become a doctor. It was inbred, natural.

She cut a cube of butter into the frying pan, then began cracking eggs into a bowl.

Nash crossed to her and she lifted her gaze.

He took an uncracked egg from her hand and put it back in the carton. She just stood there, staring, wondering what he was up to and knowing exactly what by the look in his eyes.

"No." She stepped away, but he caught her around the waist, dragging her back like a child trying to escape punishment. Then he pulled her warmly against him. All the sensations of her dream rocketed to the surface.

"Yes." Nash wrapped his arms more firmly around her, the contact making his blood flow heavy in his groin. Yet he held her gaze and saw wariness, doubt.

"The men are going to be here any second." Her hands on his bare chest, she tried pushing. It was like trying to move the earth off its axis. "It wouldn't be wise for them to find their boss with the nanny in his arms."

"Let them get their own nanny."

Her lips curved. "You're insufferable."

"I'm suffering."

Her smile fell. "Oh, Nash."

"Forgive me, baby. I know I don't deserve it, but I need it. God, so badly."

She searched his features, his crystal-blue eyes. Beneath the strong exterior lay a beast clawing to be let out of his prison, and Hayley's heart bled for him.

"Of course, I forgive you." His relief swept down his body in a hard shudder, and she realized he'd been holding his breath. "You were as much a victim as I was."

"But I could have changed it. I could have——"

"What? You thought she was carrying your child. And even if there was a shadow of doubt——" his look said there'd been more than a shadow "——you are too honorable to ignore the possibility."

He pressed his forehead to hers.

"Face it, Nash, you're one of the good guys."

A smile threatened his lips. "Say it again. Just so I know I'm not dreaming."

"I forgive you, Nashville."

"It's worth hearing that god-awful name." He kissed her forehead, holding her close, his hand rubbing her back. "Thank you, darlin'."

She laid her head to his chest, tightened her arms around his waist and sighed.

Nash knew torment and contentment in one instant. Her forgiveness gave him a divine release, exposing all he'd suppressed. He tried ignoring this energy warming between them, but he couldn't. It seeped past his clothes, into his skin, and made him realize he'd been a mom and dad so long he'd forgotten what it was like just to be a man, someone's lover. Until Hayley. The instant he saw her again, she made him remember long throbbing kisses and damp bodies rolling under the sheets; connecting physically and emotionally to another human being so closely you could feel every breath they took as if it was yours. And the longer he was near her, the stronger the need grew. He didn't want to feel it, not so completely, so quickly. Again. He kept repeating to himself that he couldn't fold under this need for her, not with the girls at risk, not even when

she was the first and only woman he'd desired with
every cell of his body.

But if Nash understood anything from the moment
those shapely legs dipped out of that dinosaur of a car,
it was that Hayley Albright was much more to him than
an old lover or a piece of his past. She was part of him.

More than just his desire for her worked through him,
and beyond the years of loneliness was the crushing
feeling that she distrusted him. It was justified, yet it
weighed heavy on his soul. He'd earned a reputation of
trust, of a man worthy of breeding million-dollar Thoroughbreds, and yet when he wanted that honor from her,
she couldn't give it. She might not say the words, but
he'd seen it her eyes.

His hand slid up to cup the back of her head, to tip
it until she met his gaze. The instant their gazes locked
everything changed. The air burned, bodies clung more
tightly. Blood moved more slowly through his veins and
his muscles locked with a sweet heat that left him in a
breathless state of hardness.

She felt it, shifting slightly against him.

Nash thought he'd come apart right there. It was too
soon to ask for a second chance. But he had to taste
her. He lowered his head.

"Oh, Nash," she said in a trembling sigh.

His name on the breathy rush undid him. He swooped
down and was suddenly powerfully, deeply in her
mouth, his tongue plundering, taking possession. He
didn't try to hide his need. He didn't need to. She drew
it from him the way a river breaks against a dam, letting
her desire rush over him, envelope him. She clawed at
his shoulders, trying to get closer, and he clutched her,
dropping to the nearby stool, pulling her between his
thighs.

A whimper escaped her throat.

He drank in that, too.

With one hand he cupped her bottom, pushing her into him. She flexed in a ribbon of desire, her breathing rushed, her hands in his hair as she tipped his head to take more of him and match it with the fire of memory. But it was hotter, stronger, more potent than she thought possible, and Hayley knew she was in real danger. Then when his hands drove up her back, under her shirt and she let him, the burn of his touch spiraled her need out of control. She wanted to be naked with him, feel his incredible mouth on her body, feel his hardness push insistently into her as his tongue pushed into her mouth now.

It had been way too long.

The sound of the front door opening broke into their privacy.

Nash groaned in frustration and pulled back slowly, kissing the corner of her mouth, her cheek.

Hayley gasped for breath, blinking, the haze slow to lift. She met his gaze and the fire smoldered, begging to be flamed again. The kiss had opened a door she wanted locked. And yet, another part of her longed to cross the threshold and throw away the key.

She staggered back. No, she couldn't do this. It was just the emotions of the night before lingering.

Nash struggled for control. His groin was unbearably thick and heavy. For her. He hadn't felt like this in years, not this lack of control, and if the men weren't coming into the house, he would have made love to her right there on the floor. He lifted his gaze to her and frowned at the look in her eyes.

His heart rolled in his chest.

Distrust, shame, laced with the sting of old hurt.

"I can't do this again," she whispered. "I won't."

His features darkened. "Hayley, things are different now." He could hear the footsteps of his men coming closer.

Her gaze narrowed.

"You can't lie to yourself and say that wasn't something," he said.

Her mouth curved bitterly. "Oh, it was something all right." Stronger, hotter, wilder than before, she thought. "But we can't start up. I'm leaving."

He wasn't going to discuss her leaving. That was less than two weeks away. "You don't trust me not to hurt you again."

She tipped her chin and gave him a cool look. "That doesn't matter."

"Of course it matters!" When she simply stared, he said, "By God, you are a stubborn woman. And we will talk about this later." The last came like a warning.

"There is nothing to discuss, Nash. I don't have a choice this time. People are depending on me."

He didn't say anything, unnerving her more as he stood. He groaned, his body too tight to walk.

A very unladylike snicker escaped her, and when she shot her a dark look, an instance of mutual heat pulsed between them. Seth strolled into the kitchen and stopped short, glancing between the two. Nash ignored him, still standing only a hand's width from her. He stared, an almost triumphant smile crossing his lips when he heard her breath hitch.

His gaze lingered, caressed and stroked her as intimately as his touch, and Hayley felt her insides twist and shudder.

"Get to cooking, woman," he growled softly. "We're burning daylight."

Hayley nodded. At least she thought she did. His stare was too intense to feel much past the delicious numbing of his kiss and the sensation of simply being looked at as if he could peel away her skin and see beneath. But he *had* seen beneath. And his look said he remembered every inch of her, every cry of passion, every push into her body and its resounding friction. It was a persuasive look, and she gloried in feeling so desired, wanting him in ways she had no business thinking about. He was devastating to her senses, his scent mixing with hers. And to top it off, his eyes were somber, glittering with something she hadn't seen in a man's eyes for a very long time—hunger. She had to get control of herself before she leaped on him, demanding he crush her in his arms again and make love to her mouth as he just had. For where Nash was concerned, she was the vulnerable one.

Five

Hayley did her best not to think about Nash.

Instead, she tried to make the day fun for the girls, playing as much as possible and skipping housework. Some things were more important than making sure the kitchen floor was clean enough to eat off of.

Such as playing a good game of jacks.

Or holding your pinky finger out while you sip make-believe tea.

Or wearing the correct length of boa feathers with the right dress.

And a hat, of course, Hayley thought as the wide-brimmed summer hat fell over her eyes. Kate giggled. Hayley pushed the hat back and extended her hand and the china cup.

"If you would be so kind, Miss Kimberly," she said, winking at the child. Kim poured, she and her sister sitting across from her under the shade on the back veranda, dolled up in musty old gowns their grandmother had left in a trunk for them to play dress-up. She herself wore a blue satin gown reminiscent of Audrey Hepburn, and a hat that belonged only at the Kentucky Derby. And though they'd been in the pool most of the morning, their bathing suits under the gowns, it was a day for silliness. And Hayley was just in the mood for it, avoiding all trains of thought that led to Nash and his claim that this time it was different. There was no "this time." She was sidestepping him and that talk he wanted to have. She didn't want to hear it, not a word. Because if she did, she just might fall for him again. And there was no chance of her delaying or giving up her dream.

Trying to change the direction of her thoughts, she shoved out of the chair. "We need to dance. All this tea makes a girl itchin' to wiggle."

The girls grinned as Hayley tuned the radio to a rock station. Kim and Kate scrambled off their chairs, singing and dancing, and Hayley laughed at the twins gyrating inside the too-large dresses, clunking around in heels. She joined the girls, adoring their little bumps and grinds. *Oh, they're going to be heartbreakers,* she thought.

"Can anyone join in or is this a private party?"

Hayley stilled and spun around to see Nash walking toward them. And what a walk it was. Did all men saunter as if they were fresh out of a spaghetti western, or only wealthy Carolina ranchers? Regardless, avoiding the man was impossible. Especially when he gave her those possessive looks that drew her insides tight. As he was now.

Determined not to let his effect on her show, she smiled. "Sure, you know the slide."

His lips quirked at the corner. "I think I can manage."

He stepped in beside her in the line dance, his smile slight, his gaze lingering on the gown his mom had worn to her high-school-graduation dance that fit Hayley in all the right places and showed off her sweet curves. He'd watched her and his daughters for a few minutes before making his presence known. It was too much fun seeing them together, being silly. He couldn't imagine Michelle getting down on the ground and playing jacks in a gown. But then, Hayley was always pretty much a free spirit. It was one of the things he'd loved about her. She was never embarrassed by doing something spontaneous or to the beat of a different drummer.

Nash smiled, aware he made her nervous. It was a new sensation, since there wasn't much that fazed her. She'd been hiding from him, and he'd given her some space. He didn't want to be a threat and he wasn't going to pressure her into anything. That was what got him into trouble before. He wanted her to understand that and relax. Any man with eyes could see how she tensed around him.

The music ended and she smiled up at him. "You always were a great dancer."

"Glad there are some good things you remember about me."

He didn't give her time to comment or remember old pain as he pulled her into his arms, spinning her across the pool deck as another song played.

The girls made noises as if they were seeing something they shouldn't.

Hayley's insides tripped, her heart jumping and reminding her how much this man could stir her with just a look. His hand was warm and sure in hers, the one around her waist like a steel band. Thighs brushed as they fell into step, dancing close and in perfect sync. He spun her out, then whipped her close to his side, and she laughed, a bright free sound he swore made the sun shine brighter.

Nash grinned when she sent the huge hat sailing into a nearby chair before their dramatic finish. The twins clapped.

"What else are you going to take off?" he said for her ears alone.

She really shouldn't, but he was asking for it, looking at her like that. It would serve him right. She stepped back and in one motion, unzipped the dress, letting it drop to her ankles. She gave him a saucy pose, then dove into the pool. The twins shrieked with laughter. Nash just stood there, stunned for a second. Hayley came up for air, smoothing her hair back and telling the girls to come join her, without the gowns.

"You should have seen your face, Daddy!" Kim shouted. "Your eyes got this big." She did an imitation that made her look like she was being strangled.

"Yeah, yeah," he said, winking at them before he squatted at the edge of the pool, gazing into Hayley's eyes as she swam to him. "I swear that one—" he nodded at the swimsuit "—is smaller than the other."

"If you don't like it, don't look."

"Honey, no man alive could resist looking at all that lovely skin."

She flushed at the compliment. "You should know never to dare me, Nash."

His muscles clamped. A memory surged. "Making love on Hunting Beach," he whispered, and her skin darkened.

"Shh." Hayley glanced at the girls, sitting on the

steps waiting for her permission to come in. She hadn't
meant to bring that up. Instantly she pushed away from
the pool ledge, diving under the water and coming up
beside the girls. She helped them into their inner tubes,
spinning them.

"Lunch is in the fridge," she called as Nash started
to walk away. She looked back over her shoulder and
met his gaze. "It's fend for yourself till dinner."

"Are you dismissing me?"

Hayley grinned. "Yeah, cowboy. Go to work."

He hooked his thumbs in his belt loops. "And if I
don't want to?"

The twins looked between the adults, nudging each
other.

"Suit yourself. You're the boss."

Nash flung off his hat and dove into the pool, clothes
and all.

"Daddy!" his daughters shrieked when he came up
beside them.

Hayley blinked. "I don't believe you did that."

He smoothed his hair back. "Why?"

"It's so not you."

"Let's get one thing straight," he growled, pushing
his daughters in their tubes to the center of the pool and
out of earshot. "Things are different. We both are."

Her guard went up, a reaction he'd come to recognize
since she'd arrived. "Nash."

"Don't go flying off again," he told her, holding
himself at a respectable distance when he wanted to
crush her in his arms. "We're both older, wiser, and I
have my children to consider. Can't we just take it as
it comes and be...friends?"

Friends. She ought to be hurt by such a bland description. But isn't that what she wanted? "Fine. That's all we are now, anyway."

That stung, but Nash masked his hurt with a smile. "If we're going to be pals, then you'd better wear a bigger bathing suit."

"If we're going to be pals, Nash, then you need to stop looking at me like you want to devour me."

He inched closer, knowing it wasn't wise. Knowing he'd destroy the truce he'd just formed with her. "But I do, baby, I do." His gaze swept her breasts, nearly spilling from the bikini top, before meeting hers. "In one bite."

Hayley inhaled and didn't have time to comment. He dove underwater and swam to the opposite end of the pool, pausing long enough to give his daughters a kiss before he strode, dripping wet, back to the house.

Hayley sank underwater, praying it cooled her hot skin.

Friends? What a crock.

Nash threw down his pen and rubbed his face. For two days he'd smothered his feelings and kept innuendo and anything misleading out of conversation with Hayley. He accepted chance meetings, meals and idle conversations with an attitude that was nothing more than friendship. It was a supreme effort, being around her, wanting her, so mostly he stayed in the corral or in the barns, working with the vet and birthing a new foal. Well, mostly he stayed away. He saw her only at dinner. She still refused to join them for meals. It upset the girls, but she carefully explained to them she was the nanny, not their mother. Nash's throat ached then, because of the catch in her voice when she said this and when she finally looked at him. The girls didn't understand and sulked until Hayley brought them root-beer floats for dessert. Five-year-olds. So easily rerouted, he thought, wishing a root-beer float did the trick for him.

Nash sighed, then racked papers and set them aside, unable to concentrate another moment. All this not wanting was driving him nuts. The house was uncomfortably silent, and just knowing she was out there somewhere sent him out of his chair. So much for restraint, he thought, leaving his office, heading to the kitchen and hoping she was in bed. Then he saw her and wondered where the woman found the energy to get up before sunrise and stay awake past nine.

Sitting in the middle of the living-room floor, she wore denim shorts and a purple tank top, her face in a medical book and a notepad beside her. Stacks of books and papers littered the floor like layers of cake waiting to be devoured. An open briefcase rested a few feet away. Quietly he backtracked to the kitchen, then returned, clearing his throat and holding up two glasses of iced tea.

"Join me?"

"Oh, that's looks great," she said with feeling, taking it as he bent. She waved him down. "Sit, you're making my neck hurt."

He folded to the floor, pulling the book from her lap and turning it to read the title.

"I thought you were done with this. Just waiting on your assignment."

"I've only completed my first year of internship. I have three more to do in my field." That brought his head up. "Since I don't have any family, I'm using my leave time to work before I go back to St. Anthony's. But I still have to test constantly before the boards. It never hurts to keep studying." She looked at all the books. "I always feel as if there's something I've missed or forgotten to study."

Nash knew differently. Hayley had a photographic memory. It was one of the traits that got her incredible grades in college and scholarships. It also made him see what a great doctor she'd make and reminded him that she wasn't sticking around. Like his wife. Hayley had her dream and he wasn't part of it. She hadn't wanted to be his wife before she had her MD, and it was what had brought them to an impasse before. But Nash told himself he was wiser for it and his mistakes. He just didn't know why he couldn't handle her decision any more than he could seven years ago. Maybe because he felt totally excluded.

"You've done great for yourself, sprite."

She looked up from her notes.

"I admire your fortitude. Anyone else would have given up such an arduous task when they knew it would take two years longer than the norm."

Warmth spread through her and she smiled. "Thanks, Nash. That means a lot to me." It meant everything.

"You've done well with my house, too, especially since ten years ago it had a staff of five," he said.

Her brows shot up at that. "Maybe you should pay me more, then?" she said with a smile.

"Gladly. I've never seen my girls so happy."

Her expression turned tender and loving. "They're great kids."

For a second they stared, need and want and the denial of it mirrored in their eyes. The sensations passing between them had nothing to do with what they once were to each other. And everything to do with that they could be.

Nash warned himself to tread carefully and said,

"How about I quiz you?" He pulled the book close and reclined on his side.

Hayley eyed him for a second, then leaned over and pointed to the chapter. Nash glanced, then formed questions, one after another. He flipped to a sample test and quizzed her. They sipped tea and halfway through the studying he left to bring back a snack for her and a beer for himself.

Two hours later she was slumped on the floor, yawning between responses.

Nash closed the book. "Bedtime, Hayley. Right now."

Her eyes closed and she smiled sleepily. "You like giving me orders way too much, Rayburn."

"Hell, yeah. This is the only time I ever could and you'll do it."

She met his gaze. "I never had anyone tell me what to do, not even my dad when he was alive. He was glad I just kept myself busy and out of trouble."

That neglect bred an independent woman who was afraid to get close to anyone, he thought. And afraid to relinquish any responsibility for her survival to another.

She lay back and stretched like a cat, arching her back, and Nash wanted to crawl over and feel her flesh beneath his palms, his mouth.

As if she'd read his thoughts, she instantly sat up, gathered her papers and books, then stuffed them into the briefcase.

Nash stood, and when she went to pick up the dishes, he stopped her. "I'll get them. Go on to bed."

He was close, gazing into her clear brown eyes, his fingers wrapped around her elbow.

"Thanks. Good night."

"Night."

He didn't move.

Neither did she.

It took every effort to keep his muscles still, to not relent to the messages his brain was sending, to bend and take her sweet mouth with his. He held her gaze the way a prisoner seeks a key to freedom, wondering if there was any escape and wondering whether the release would be worth more time in his own jail. He hadn't been with many women since Michelle died. He hadn't wanted to. Women he'd dated were just people, nothing setting them apart from one another. Nash knew even if he'd just met Hayley, he would feel the same unending need to be with her.

God, this was harder than he thought.

And sex wasn't everything.

Trust was more. He let her go and stepped back.

"Night."

"See you at sunrise." She lifted her briefcase and headed for the hall, leaving him alone with his thoughts.

"Nashville Davis Rayburn!"

Nash cringed at the power of her voice and his full name filtering through the breeding barn. He looked over the horse's back.

"You bellowed, Miss Albright?"

She made a face at him, her hands on her hips. "Why didn't you tell me the twins were going to their grandmother's for the week?"

Nash shrugged, pulling the horse into the stall. "Slipped my mind."

"Your daughters are leaving, them being the reason you hired me, I might add, and it slipped your mind?"

"Yes, Hayley, it did." Stooping, he checked the animal's legs. "I have an international auction to prepare for. People will be coming and going for the next several days, getting starting bids, categorizing stock. I simply forgot. The girls usually spend *two* weeks with my mom around this time of year.''

She cocked her head. ''Then you don't need me anymore.''

His insides clenched. ''Far from it.'' He straightened, meeting her gaze. ''I still need a cook and a housekeeper.''

''But—''

He gave her a bland look, all business right now. ''Is that a problem?''

''No, it's just that—''

''The girls were a nice barrier, right? You didn't have to deal with me directly with them between us.''

''That's not true.'' It was and she knew it.

He ducked under the horse's neck, pausing to secure the leads to the bridle before he faced her. ''Are you afraid to be alone with me?''

She scoffed, meeting his gaze. ''You are the last person who scares me, Nash.''

''Good, then we can just relax.''

Relax. Right. If she was any more relaxed, she'd snap in two.

''Okay, so what do they need me to pack for them?''

''Why don't you call Mom and ask?''

''No.''

He frowned. ''Why not?''

''Because, well, you know—'' she waved distractedly ''—she knows about us.''

He smirked. ''I thought you weren't afraid?''

She wasn't. Not at all. Except that getting to know his mother, his family, was stepping over the line. Especially if she wanted to keep the lines clear. ''Okay, fine. I'll call.'' She did an about-face and strode down the long corridor between the stalls. ''But if she asks, I'm gonna tell her all the things you did when you were living in Georgia.''

''The things I did or *we* did?''

She stopped short, then threw a look back over her shoulder.

He grinned.

''Then again, I ought to ask her all the things you did before we met.''

''Go right ahead. I have no secrets.'' Not anymore, he thought.

Her brow worked for a second before she turned away.

His mother didn't know she was here. And Nash was looking forward to the moment when the two women met. And hoping he gained an ally.

They were ganging up on her.

''Nash's Hayley? Hayley Albright?'' The shock in Mrs. Rayburn's voice made Hayley smile.

''Yes, ma'am,'' she said into the phone.

''I thought you were a doctor.''

''I am. I'm working through my leave time before I continue my residency.''

''Oh.'' A pause and then, ''You didn't know this Wife Incorporated assignment was at River Willow, did you?''

The sympathy in her tone touched a needy spot in Hayley. ''No, ma'am.''

''Bet that was a shock.'' She laughed, a rich sound, as if she did it often.

''Oh, you could say that. I think Kat Davenport was playing matchmaker.''

"She always did have a devilish streak, that girl. How is she, by the way?"

"Doing well. I haven't actually laid eyes on her in about seven months, ma'am."

"Stop ma'aming me, Hayley. Makes me feel ancient. Call me Grace."

Hayley relaxed for the first time since she'd dialed Nash's mother's phone number. "Okay, Grace, give me a rough idea of what I need to pack for the twins." Hayley listened and made a list. The girls came into the kitchen, and when they started to talk, Hayley motioned to the phone, then told them to hush before she went back to writing. "Got it. Tomorrow morning after breakfast. Sure, no problem. They're dancing around me right now."

Hayley handed Kate the phone and the pair, their faces pressed together, talked to their grandmother. They asked a dozen questions and made plans as Hayley went into the laundry room to do another load and make certain their jeans were clean for taking to Grace's place.

"She's so cool, Grandma," Kate said.

"We played dress-up and went swimming, and tonight we get to have a bubble bath," Kim said as if they'd be getting gold, instead of getting wet.

Hayley turned on the washer, not wanting to hear what the girls said, not wanting to love them, but she knew it was hopeless. She adored them, and knowing they'd be gone tomorrow made her throat constrict. She wouldn't get to see them again before she left for St. Anthony's hospital.

"Miss Hayley?"

She turned. Kim held out the phone. Hayley took it, saying, "Anything else we need to know?"

"Other than that my granddaughters are happy, not a thing. See you in the morning."

Hayley said goodbye and hung up. Butterflies started jumping in her stomach.

Meeting Mrs. Grace Rayburn wasn't the problem. Being alone in this house for another week with her son was.

The next morning Kim and Kate raced through the house, skidding to a halt in the kitchen. "Morning, Miss Hayley!" they chimed.

"There's my ladies," Hayley said happily, squatting as the girls launched themselves into her arms, wrapping her in bone-crushing hugs. "Oh, what a way to start a day!"

They giggled and when they pulled back, she told them to go into the dining area off the kitchen, and she'd bring them their breakfast.

"But we want to be in here with you."

The innocent statement touched Hayley deeply, and she swallowed around the knot in her throat. She lifted them each onto a stool, then gave them their breakfast, flipping on the small TV on the counter so they could watch cartoons. While they ate, Hayley cleaned up the breakfast mess from nearly a dozen men, and by the time the girls finished, so was she.

"Go wash up and dress in the clothes I laid out," she told them. As they hurried off in a whirlwind of pink nightgowns, she called, "Brush your teeth and bring down a comb and barrettes so I can put up all that hair."

Hayley slumped on the stool, slapping a dish towel over her shoulder. She'd spent yesterday evening cooking dinner, running bubble baths and avoiding that "I'm going to be alone with you'' look Nash kept throwing her way. Which was why she said she'd take care of everything for the twins. At least their cute little pink-and-navy-plaid suitcases were already packed and by the door, with their stuffed bears and dolls and everything else little girls needed to survive in a room that wasn't their own.

"A handful, huh?"

Hayley looked up.

Nash's mom.

Hayley smiled. "Yeah, are you sure you want this chaos for two weeks?" Hayley wondered how long the woman had been standing there.

Grace waved the remark off, walking into the kitchen. She wasn't any more than fifty-five and stunning. Her short haircut was chic and swept to one side, showing off the silver streak in her brown hair. Though she wore jeans and a red blouse, she was a woman who took good care of herself, minding the tiny details that make men look twice and other women envy.

She smiled, giving Hayley a bold once-over, then saying, "Let's talk, honey."

Hayley offered her a cup of coffee and poured one for herself. They sat at the counter across from each other.

"I knew what you looked like. He's got a snapshot in his wallet, though it went through the wash once."

That was obviously how Grace knew the photo was there, Hayley thought, the center of her chest tightening. She had one of Nash, too, tucked in the lining of her suitcase. Hayley met her gaze. "Grace, let's be honest. No matter what you might be thinking, I'm here, working for Wife Incorporated because the money is great. I have a career to get back to, and Nash and the girls deserve more. And I don't fit in here. Besides, we agreed to be friends.''

Grace nodded, at home with her honesty. "Okay, then let me say one thing."

Hayley smiled. "Just one?"

"For now."

"Shoot."

"My son made a big mistake years ago." Grace lowered her voice. "Give him a chance."

"I forgave him, Grace."

Grace's brows drew down and she tipped her head slightly, studying Hayley. "You know it all?"

"I believe so, yes."

"I guess if you're still here, it says something."

"It says that I stick to my obligations."

"Is that what those three are, obligations?"

Hayley looked at her coffee. "Of course not." Those three had suddenly become a glaring marker in her life and a wedge in her heart. She couldn't seem to go forward. She looked at Grace. "I'm leaving. I have to. I don't want you to think there's something here that will alter that. There is just no way."

Grace absorbed this. At least, Hayley thought she did, and she knew she sounded cold.

The moment passed and Hayley launched into questions about Grace's place, and they discussed the ranch and the girls, skipping politely past Michelle and on to Nash.

"This auction is the biggest event of his year."

"I gathered that. I'll do what I can to help."

"You two talking about me?"

Hayley jerked around. Man, did he look good. A body didn't have the right to have so much sex appeal. "God, Nash, your ego is way too big."

He strolled inside, walking to his mother and planting a kiss on her cheek. "You look great, Mom."

Grace eyed him. "So do you. At least it looks as if you're eating better."

He patted his flat stomach. "Hayley's cooking."

Grace glanced between the two as they stared at each other.

Hayley noticed Grace's interest and sent her "forget it" look just as the girls arrived, hair flying. After they hugged their grandmother, Hayley excused herself to go braid their hair.

"Well?" Nash said when he and his mom were alone.

Grace's eyes were still on Hayley as she escorted the girls into the guest bathroom. Finally she met her son's gaze. "That's one scared woman, Nash."

"I know."

She gave him a playful smack on the shoulder.

"Ow. What did I do now?"

"That's for letting her get away."

He smiled down at his mother. "Not this time."

She frowned back. "I don't think you'll have a choice, honey."

"Everyone has a choice, Mom."

Six

"If I have to drag you in there and feed you myself, Hayley, I will," Nash said, trying to keep his temper out of his voice and low enough that the ranch hands sitting in the dining room wouldn't hear.

"I double dare you." She smiled.

He wasn't amused and leaned closer. "Don't tempt me."

"You can be such a tyrant."

"I'm your boss."

She reared back. "Is that an order?"

He sighed, pushing his fingers through his hair. She was so stubborn. "Of course not, but you've been moping around since the girls left."

"I have not."

He eyed her, though he was touched that she missed them as much as he did.

She sighed. "All right, so what if I am? I don't have a lot to do without them around."

"Any other woman would be enjoying the free time. Why don't you take a break?"

She glanced in the direction of the dining room. "Having supper with y'all…it's not right."

"It's my house and I say it is."

She had to give him that and she did feel more alone without the girls around. "Okay, fine. No one can ever call me a party pooper."

Spinning around, she walked into the dining room with Nash behind her. There were three extra ranch hands she hadn't met before, and every one of them stood when she entered the room. Jimmy Lee rushed around the table to pull out her chair.

Nash eyed him back to his seat as Hayley sat down.

It was strange being in here with all of them. She'd made it a point when she took a job like this not to join in the meals. But after a quick comical prayer, they dug in and made her feel welcome. They discussed plans for the auction, and Nash assigned duties for the next few days. Hayley made mental notes to keep quick meals and sandwiches around for them since they weren't on their normal routine. Rounding up all the horses grazing on more than a thousand acres would take a while, and she needed to be prepared. She passed a dinner platter, glancing up to find Nash staring at her from the opposite end of the table. She lifted her chin and motioned for him to mind his own plate. He simply stared and she could feel the message down the length of table. He wanted her there, and the small fact scared the hell out of her.

Nash relaxed in his chair, eating, but not really tasting the incredible meal she'd prepared. Watching her was far more interesting. That and listening to her draw out Bubba and refusing to call him anything but Robert. Pride seeped through him. She'd told his mother she didn't fit in, but here she was, making every man hang on her words. She asked about their hobbies, interests, their families, their homes, and Nash heard a little envy in her voice, yet she held nothing back, teasing Ronnie about his long hair and treating Beau like a man when he was scarcely out of high school. When she stood to get the water pitcher, Beau leaped to her aid. She had them at her command and Nash was a willing soldier.

"That was great, as usual, Hayley." Nash gestured to the empty platters and bowls on the table.

She smiled, her fingers steepled under her chin even as she accepted compliments from the men. "Y'all still have room? I made dessert."

Good grief, he thought, when?

She went into the kitchen and came back with peach cobbler and a chocolate cream pie. At the sideboard, she dished up the cobbler and set a plate before Nash. He stared at the cobbler, then lifted his gaze to her.

"You remembered." It was his favorite.

Twisting slightly, she winked, then turned back to the sideboard to serve up the rest.

When the hands stood up to leave, each offered compliments, saying they were glad to finally dine with her.

She beamed, then started to collect the dishes. Nash helped.

"I have it," she said.

"So do I," he said in a no-nonsense tone. Hayley shrugged and went to the kitchen. Nash brought in the rest of the dishes, tossing the linens into the laundry room as she washed and rinsed, filling the dishwasher and scrubbing pots.

He leaned against the counter behind her, watching her. A delightful pastime lately.

"Don't you have work to do?" she said without turning around.

"No, I wanted to ask you something."

She glanced over her shoulder. "What?"

"Will you go to the auction with me day after tomorrow?"

"Me?" She turned, water dripping off her sponge. She immediately tossed it into the sink and wiped up the mess. "Why?" Oh, this shouldn't make her so nervous.

"Because I want you to see it, understand what I do."

"I know what you do." She turned back to the sink. "You talked of nothing but this ranch while you were in Georgia working for that stock brokerage." She shook her head, bending to put the last dish in the dishwasher. "Why you worked there in the first place was beyond me."

"I was supposed to be sowing my wild oats." His tone was dry. "Dad thought I should get off the ranch before spending a lifetime here." Nash had been twenty-eight at the time and his father hadn't realized how much sowing he'd already done. Until he met Hayley. He knew then he was finished. A little pang of regret slid through him. He pushed it aside. *That was then and this is now,* he thought. "You never said anything."

She glanced at him. "I wanted you around, yet I remember the look in your eyes when you talked about the plantation. Seeing it, I understood."

Nash smiled, moving toward her, loving how her

eyes got a little darker and her stance a little softer. "So, Dr. Albright. Can you handle a day or two with me?"

"Won't you be busy?"

He shook his head. "That's why all the buyers come here beforehand. They know what the top-dollar mark is and a horse doesn't go for less that he's worth. Unless there's more than one buyer, then the real fun starts. I might sell them all. I might not. That's the gamble."

She gazed up at him and ignored the voices screaming, *No, don't do it,* for she really wanted to go. She couldn't remember the last time she'd been out anywhere with anyone. And she wanted to see the auction. *Yeah,* she thought. *Keep telling yourself it's horses you want to hang out with and maybe you'll convince yourself.*

"What do you say?"

"What do I wear?"

"Boots and jeans. It's not exactly the Kentucky Derby."

She nodded.

He was so pleased he wanted to kiss the daylights out of her, but the word *trust* blew through his mind just then.

"It lasts for a couple of days. There's a rodeo, trick riders, a cattle auction, too."

"Anything else I should now about this event?"

He was thoughtful for a moment. "The people from the auction houses will be here tomorrow."

Her eyes widened. "When?"

"After breakfast, I 'spect."

She inhaled and shoved him back. "Good Lord, Nash! You didn't think to tell me this?" She closed the dishwasher and flipped it on.

"What's the big deal?"

"A houseful of people before noon!" She had to prepare something and clean up more. In the center of the
kitchen, she shifted impatiently on her feet, not knowing
exactly what to do first.

"Chill out, honey. They're coming to look at horses,
not inspect the house."

She sent him an irritated look. "Oh, just like a man,"
she groused, then headed toward her room. "Didn't
your mama teach you about Southern hospitality?"

"Apparently not enough," he said to the empty
kitchen.

Representatives of the auction house arrived just after
breakfast. They were here to inspect horseflesh for starting bids for the auction this coming weekend. Hayley
left a light brunch laid out in the dining room, and without the girls around to keep her busy, she acted as a
hostess for Nash. She felt his gaze follow her as she
refilled one man's cup, and he stared so hard and long
she felt her skin heat.

She glanced to the side, the silver carafe in her hand.
She was suddenly conscious of her simple teal tank
dress that had seen one too many washings. In a slow
saunter, Nash moved toward her, his every step sending
a spark of anticipation through her.

"Thank you," he whispered. "You didn't have to do
this."

She shrugged. "You want the best price, don't you?"

He smiled, his gaze wandering over her upturned
face. This morning when he'd found his dining room
draped in old family linens and set as elegantly as his
mother would have done, Nash was knocked to his
knees by the gesture. In the year and half that Michelle
was his wife, she hadn't bothered to do anything like

Come closer still to Silhouette with two **FREE** books and a welcome gift

How to claim your two FREE books and welcome gift

If you've enjoyed reading this new book, then this is your opportunity to get ever closer still to Silhouette Desire™ and enjoy two more free books and a welcome gift. This is all you have to do.

1. **Peel off the free gift seal** from the front cover. Place it in the space provided to the right. This automatically entitles you to receive two free books and a lovely silvertone heart necklace.

2. **Complete your details** on the card, detach it along the dotted line, and post it back to us. No stamp needed. We'll then send you two selected romances from the Desire™ series, yours to keep absolutely FREE.

3. **Enjoy the read.** We hope that after receiving your free books you'll want to remain a subscriber. But the choice is yours – to continue or cancel, any time at all! So why not accept our no risk invitation. You'll be glad you did.

Your satisfaction is guaranteed

You are under no obligation to buy anything. We charge you nothing for your introductory parcel. And you don't have to make any minimum number of purchases – not even one! Thousands of readers have already discovered that the Reader Service™ is the most convenient way of enjoying the latest new romance novels before they are available in the shops. Of course, post and packing to your home is completely FREE.

Jane Nicholls

Yours FREE...
when you reply today

This elegant necklace is classically styled with an exquisite heart pendant presented on a generous 46cm (18") silvertone chain. Respond today and it's all yours.

YES. Please send me my two FREE books and welcome gift

Welcome to Silhouette

FREE GIFT SEAL

YES. I have placed my free gift seal in the space provided above. Please send me two free books and my welcome gift. I understand that I am under no obligation to purchase any books, as explained on the back and on the opposite page. I am over 18 years of age.

BLOCK CAPITALS

D1FI

Ms/Mrs/Miss/Mr _____ Initials _____

Surname _____

Address _____

_____

_____ Postcode _____

Thank you!

Detach and keep your complimentary bookmark ▶

How The Silhouette® Reader Service™ works

Accepting free books and gifts places you under no obligation to buy anything. You may keep the books and gift and return the despatch note marked "cancel". If we don't hear from you, about a month later we will send you four new novels and invoice you for just £2.80* each. That's the complete price – there is no extra charge for postage and packing. You may cancel at any time, otherwise every month we'll send you four more books which you may purchase or return – the choice is yours.

*Terms and prices subject to change without notice.

SILHOUETTE READER SERVICE
FREE BOOK OFFER
FREEPOST CN81
CROYDON
CR9 3WZ

If this offer card is missing, please write to: The Reader Service, P.O. Box 236, Croydon, Surrey CR9 3RU

NO
STAMP
NEEDED

that, though the auction was a twice-yearly event. Hayley had a talent for making the officials feel comfortable enough to tell her things about themselves and their families even Nash didn't know. And he'd been working with these people for years. Good bedside manner for the future, he thought, and disliked the reminder that she'd be leaving soon.

"Buttering up never hurt," she said, leaning close so they were not heard.

She refilled his coffee. Nash stared at her bowed head, catching the scent of her perfume. Her nearness excited him beyond rational thought. She tipped her head, her dark gaze clashing with his, and he could almost feel the current crackling between them. Casually, he laid his hand on her waist and heard her indrawn breath.

It was the first time he'd touched her since they'd danced by the pool. His fingers flexed, tugging her an inch or two closer, and the memory of her bare skin beneath his hands instantly brought another time when he'd made her gasp for air. And how he'd done it. He wanted to do it again and again and could scarcely control the images colliding through his mind. He bent to whisper, "You look lovely this morning, sprite."

Her cheeks brightened becomingly. "Thanks."

His voice dropped to a sensual timbre. "Downright delectable."

A little sound, close to a whimper, escaped her. "Behave."

The temptation to touch her further, to sweep his arms around her and pull her close, nearly overcame him. He was grateful she stepped back before he did something foolish. He felt like one of the stallions in his barns, and it would not do his reputation any good if he laid his daughters' nanny across the two-hundred-year-old polished dining table and made love to her. The decadent thought made him chuckle softly, and her gaze flew to his.

As if she read his mind, she rolled her eyes and shook her head. He took a final sip of coffee, then set the cup aside. "Time to make some money," he said for her ears only, then urged the men and women outside.

For the remainder of the afternoon, Hayley kept busy cleaning up after the brunch while Nash presented his best stock. At last she realized there was nothing left to do except maybe polish silver, and she went to her room to study. She picked up a book and sat by the window, but never opened it, her attention drawn to the activity outside. And to Nash. She admitted she liked watching him work. Heck, she liked looking at him doing nothing. Her heart jumped a little when he led the black stallion out of the barn. He wasn't wearing his usual blue jeans and work shirt, but black jodhpurs and tall black boots. His white shirt was collarless with knife-edge creases on the sleeves. She ought to know—she'd ironed it. He led the stallion around the ring. The animal pranced regally for him, the representatives for the auction houses trailing him like puppies, clipboards in their hands. Nash commanded the beast and the people around him. His ranch hands brought the mares and foals out. Nash gestured for one pair to be led back into the barn. A representative questioned him, obviously admiring that mare in particular and wanting it in the auction. Nash shook his head and the objection ended there.

Her chin in her palm, elbow on the windowsill, she admired the man in his element. He dealt well with "corporates," people owning race horses or wanting to, as well as the Florida and Georgia cattle ranchers buying trained cutting horses from him. And Nash was a bit of both, refinement and rawhide.

And in the privacy of her mind she admitted that she envied him, his life. He lived hard, worked hard and had roots that went back two hundred years. He was comfortable doing the same job his ancestors had, day in and day out. It was that lineage, this life, that she couldn't be in. She didn't know about family or making a home. Stability and longevity were Nash Rayburn, not her. How could he have ever believed she was capable of being a wife and mother when she'd seen neither in her own life? Right now she was only an old lover with lingering memories. She couldn't expect more. And she wouldn't.

Hayley felt the sting of regret in the back of her throat. She'd tried giving him all she could give years ago and it hadn't been enough. She looked at the *Physician's Desk Reference* in her hand, then to the other books stacked on the bed. She had her plans and he had his. She didn't know a thing about his life-style other than it was beyond her. She just wouldn't fit in. It wasn't as if he'd asked her to, either, she thought. *Then why am I looking at what I cannot have as if it's the last morsel of food on the table?*

Just before she turned away from the window, she stole one last glance at him.

Over the distance his gaze locked with hers.

Hayley felt electrified. His lips curved and, astride the bareback horse, he had the creature dip his head and put out one gleaming hoof toward her.

She clapped silently.

He bowed, slight and elegant. Hayley just laughed to herself and shook her head.

Charming. The prince of River Willow with mud on his boots.

Seven

Nash shook Andrew's hand, smiling, then turned toward Hayley, drawing her forward. "Andrew Pike, I'd like you to meet Dr. Hayley Albright."

Hayley spared a look at Nash and sellers, but his attention was on Andrew. He'd been introducing her to the buyers all day as Dr. Albright, and each time it made her go warm and fuzzy inside.

Andrew, a big strapping man with a mustache, smiled, pumping her hand. "How do, doc?"

She smiled back. "I do right fine, Mr. Pike."

"Call me Andy, please. Only my secretary calls me Mister." He didn't hide his appreciation and looked his fill of her. "Dang, I can't believe I'm wishing I'd get sick." His gaze slid to Nash, then back to Hayley.

"Be careful what you wish for, Andy," Nash said.

Andrew winked at Hayley, and Nash put his arm

around her waist. She couldn't help sinking into him a little. It felt so good.

Nash noticed and his smile widened. "You going to clean me out again, Andy?"

"You do have some fine-looking horseflesh this year, as usual. How many cutters?"

"A hundred."

Hayley's brows shot up.

"I 'spect I better get to looking before they're all gone. Ma'am." Andy tipped his hat to her and she nodded, watching him make his way through the crowd.

"A hundred? I didn't know you had that many to sell."

He urged her in the opposite direction, toward a booth. "They've been delivered to the stockyard all week. The ones we rounded up will go into training. The Thoroughbreds won't be auctioned till later. Ranchers from all over the country come to Aiken to buy and sell horses at this livestock fair." He stopped before a booth, plucking a cowboy hat from the racks surrounding the stand. After a quick inspection, he dropped it on her head.

"I don't need this." Nor could she afford it.

"Your nose is already getting red."

She looked in the mirror set near a stack of hats. The cowboy hat was straw with a brown band and not so big that she looked ridiculous. When she looked back at Nash, he was waving off the change from the vendor. The vendor thanked him by name and they moved away.

Hayley said, "Thank you, but I don't need your gifts."

He knew she'd balk. "I know. But if you've noticed, you're the only one here not wearing one."

She glanced around. He was right; even the children wore hats.

"Besides, you look cute in it."

She blushed and he gave her hand a quick squeeze. Then he cocked his head, listening to an announcement. "Come on. The trick riders are going to start." He pulled her along, forgetting that her legs were a lot shorter than his, and when she tugged him back, out of breath, he apologized and met her pace.

She stopped before the bleachers. "There doesn't look to be any seats left."

He didn't hear her apparently and made his way around the bleachers. They walked beyond the security guard into the grandstand building. The ushers and guards merely nodded to him and stepped back, holding the door open. Icy conditioned air instantly chilled her skin. They walked into a carpeted area, and he led her up a chrome-railed spiral staircase to what looked like a large nightclub. There was a perfect view of the arena through massive windows tinted against the glaring sun; the box seats jutted out over the grandstand, so they'd miss nothing. Waiters moved through the small clusters of people, offering canapés and champagne.

Nash introduced her to everyone as Dr. Albright, and beyond that her presence with him obviously garnered curiosity and surprise, everything else felt like a blur. She would never recall all those names, she thought.

"Welcome back, Mr. Rayburn," a man in a Western-style tuxedo said. He ushered them into a private area near the glass windows, plucking a Reserved sign off the small table, then motioning to a waiter. She couldn't help notice that the sign was embossed with Nash's name and his plantation's.

Hayley dropped into a sofa. Not wanting to look like

a yokel, she tried not to stare at the huge crystal chandelier above her head, the closed-circuit TV, the carts of desserts or the elegantly dressed people, who looked as if they hadn't stepped out of this private club all day.

Sitting on the sofa beside her, Nash tossed his hat on a nearby chair. She followed suit, absorbing her surroundings as a waiter came forward, offering flutes of champagne. Nash took two, handing one to Hayley.

She sipped, watching the riders circle the arena. She was fascinated by the young girl standing on her horse's rump. Incredible balance, Hayley thought as they took a jump.

"Comfortable?"

She met Nash's gaze. "This is all very lovely."

His brows drew down. "I know you, Hayley. I hear a 'but' in that comment. Give."

"It's nothing really. I just feel drastically underdressed."

"You look great." He shifted closer to her, setting the flute aside. "Don't worry. I thought you'd like a break from the sun."

"I do, thank you." He was so damn handsome her heart jumped every time she looked at him, but right now she was seeing Nashville Davis Rayburn, millionaire. Even if he didn't normally show it off, this private box, the plush surroundings, screamed it at her. She would have been content in the bleachers, eating hot dogs and drinking beer, while he was comfortable with champagne and canapés and waiters in white jackets. He'd earned it, she knew, but just the same, it made the differences between them all the more apparent.

He was caviar. She was a pig-in-a-blanket.

She smiled at the thought.

"Hayley, honey." He slung his arm over the back of the sofa, effectively creating privacy. "What's wrong?"

"Nothing."

He gripped her chin with a thumb and forefinger, gazing into her eyes. "I can feel it. What's bothering you?"

When he looked at her like that, her deepest secrets could spill out without restraint. "I'm glad we came. It gives me a chance to really know your world."

He reared back a bit. "My world? You act like it's Mount Olympus or something."

She smiled again. "Close."

He let go of her chin, brushing the backs of his fingers across her cheek. Nash saw this place through her eyes, saw the wealth and money she'd never had. Damn. He'd never known anything to rattle her cage, but this had. Even if she tried to hide it. And though he didn't want her to think she wasn't welcome or that he was in any way ashamed of her, the move had backfired.

"Listen to me, honey. Those people—" he inclined his head to the groups behind him "—aren't my friends. Most of them have never set foot in a barn, let alone a place like River Willow. My friends are people like Andrew."

Hayley blinked, shocked that he knew her feelings.

"I don't mind this." She waved at the elegant surroundings. "Don't get me wrong—what woman minds being treated like a princess? But it seems so…detached."

"Snotty, you mean."

"Well…"

He took the champagne flute from her and set it aside, then stood, holding out his hand.

"Come on, Dr. Albright. Let's blow this pop stand."

She smiled and rose, picking up her hat. They left, but they didn't go to the bleachers. Nash led her up onto the fence rail, and they sat there, eating hot dogs, sipping beer and watching the show.

Hayley loved it.

Nash knew it.

Then a dark-haired man stopped by them. "Hey, Nash, you gonna join us this year?"

Nash jumped down, helping Hayley to the ground before he spoke. "I hadn't planned on it."

Hayley dumped their trash and wiped her hands as the man said, "Come on, pal. Chris Kramer broke his ankle and Dodd's wife is having a baby. We could use the extra body."

Hayley looked between the two men. Nash introduced her to Royce, and though he tipped his hat to her, he was intent on getting Nash to do something.

"I'm with a guest," Nash said.

Hayley touched his arm. "Whatever it is, Nash, go do it if you want. I'll be fine."

"You sure?"

Her hands on her hips, she gave him a "get real" look. "I've been on my own for a while, Rayburn. I think I can handle this."

He grinned. "Okay, see ya in a few." He gave her a quick kiss, helped her back up onto the rail, then patted a platform close to it. "Stay right here so I can find you."

She could feel his almost childlike excitement and laughed to herself as he took off like a shot with Royce. She shifted onto the short platform, her feet hanging over the edge. Beside her sat several girls wearing banners diagonally across their chest. Rodeo princesses, she thought. They were young and pretty and flirting with the cowboys walking past. Hayley grinned when one young man tried making a pass at her, until one of the girls told him she was Nash Rayburn's woman. The kid looked as if he'd committed a sin and tipped his hat to her. Nash Rayburn's woman. Hayley scoffed. Boy, was that sexist. Not that it didn't feel good to hear it, but she knew she was taking far more pleasure in that than she ought.

Music blared as the trick riders left the arena, and she searched the area for Nash. She listened to the garbled announcement, then asked the girl beside her. A competition, she said, a rodeo decathlon of sorts. First a barrel race, then roping and tying off a calf, ending with bronc riding. Hayley's heart started to pound as she scanned the riders lining up. There were only five of them. And one was Nash.

Oh, mercy, no.

Men and horses filed out into the huge arena. Nash was closest to her. Royce was next to him and they shook hands. Then Nash lifted his gaze to hers and smiled. She waved, a strange sense of pride swimming through her. His horse pranced. He was by far the best-looking man out there. He was in it for the fun of it, she realized, because if he wasn't, the animal beneath him would have been one of his own mounts. And he'd have practiced.

The gun went off and so did the horses. Nash was in his glory right now, she thought. He came in second, after Royce. Nash laughed and shook hands with the winner before he glanced back at her and shrugged sheepishly.

A few minutes later the attendant released a calf into the arena. Royce went after it, snagging the animal with

a lariat and taking him down. Nash was the last man
out. He hardly chased the calf, snapping the rope around
its neck, sliding to the ground, and had four legs tied
in seconds. He hopped to his feet, his hands in the air.
The crowd roared, then in another second, when his
time flashed on the big digital screen, the crowd howled
again.

"I suppose that's a good time?" Hayley said to the
girl beside her, applauding him.

The girl looked at Hayley as if appalled that she
didn't know. "Nash Rayburn has never been beat. Not
in five years."

Hayley swung her gaze back at Nash. He tipped his
hat to her, then released the calf.

When the bronc riding began, her fear climbed as
each man took to the field. The horses were merciless,
kicking and bucking the first three men off. The third
rider got his hand caught in the saddle rope when he
was thrown, and the horse dragged him, slapping him
against its side. This was nuts, Hayley thought as the
young man hit the ground with a teeth-jarring thud. The
girl beside her screamed his name and didn't relax until
he stood up and strode back to the pens.

Royce held on for six seconds and then was thrown,
hitting the fence. Moments passed before he shook himself and climbed to his feet, obviously disgusted with
his performance.

Then it was Nash's turn. The crowd hushed. Across
the dirt ring, he met Hayley's gaze, grinning in the face
of her worry.

Hayley's heart thundered as he tried controlling the
horse inside the chute. The door flung open and he
bolted forward. *Oh, God, he's going to break his neck,*
she thought, watching him get bounced up and down.

Yet he held on, his hand high in the air and a huge grin on his face. The crowd counted down the time to eight seconds. Nash held on, the black devil nearly upending himself to get him off. Hayley smothered the scream curling up her throat.

The buzzer sounded. Nash flung himself off the horse and the roadies corralled the animal back into the pen.

The announcer proclaimed him the winner.

Hayley was on the edge of her seat, battling between wanting to bust his chops for risking his life and being so proud of him.

She shouted his name, pride winning hands down. He looked at her, then started walking toward her. She leaped off the rail and ran to him, jumping into his outstretched arms.

"You fool!" she said above the noise. "You could have been hurt!"

"Nah," he said, lifting her off her feet and spinning her around. "What kind of breeder would I be if I let an old paint like that best me?"

"That was incredible!"

He stared down at her excited face and knew he couldn't stop himself.

He kissed her, wildly, passionately holding her head, the motion knocking off her hat as he took her mouth while thousands watched.

The crowd whistled and howled. The announcer made some comment she didn't hear above the roaring in her ears. She looped her arms around his neck and Nash staked his claim on her, the kiss lush and hot and way too short for his liking. He pulled back, loving her blush, loving the way she shoved at his shoulder and gave him a chiding look that didn't have much weight behind it. He didn't set her down and, instead, swept her up into his arms and carried her off the field.

She was beet red with embarrassment and buried her face in his shoulder. "Put me down."

"Nope." His gaze clashed with hers. "I like having you wrapped around me."

Hayley wanted to heed the warnings going off in her head, but she ignored them and admitted, "I like it, too."

He stopped, releasing her legs and letting her slide down the length of his body. He was still breathing hard and having her so close increased it. He didn't want to say anything that would sending her running. He had a feeling she'd been near that point earlier, so he simply smiled. "Good, 'cause we fit right nice." He kissed her again, quickly and possessively, then put his arm around her waist and led her out of the arena.

A young roadie raced up with her hat, handing it to her and congratulating Nash. He thanked the boy by name and the boy beamed. Nash's friends and employees came up to him, and he accepted congratulations and teasing over their kiss as they worked their way to a vendor stand. He bought cold drinks, and Hayley watched him drain a bottle of water, then take out a handkerchief to wipe the dust and sweat from his face and throat.

"I'm too old for that," he confided.

"You looked good. The girls beside me were drooling over you."

"Right. Like they'd drool over their father."

She scoffed at his modesty, holding his gaze. "The twins would have enjoyed seeing that."

He smiled tenderly. How like her to think of them. "They videotape it, so we can get a copy for them."

"Great. Then they can see how you could have gotten killed."

He simply smiled, pulling her close and walking with her toward the auction tents. "You worry too much, Doc." He looked down at her, pressing his lips to the top of her head. "But thanks."

The Thoroughbred auction was before dusk and an amazing thing to see. The animals were paraded in front of the buyers, and though the bidders were registered and the horses numbered in a catalog, Hayley listened as the bids rose. She could buy a mansion for the price. With a pen she marked the program listing Nash's horses, reading about him, the ribbons and the races his horses had won. A Kentucky Derby and two Preakness winners in the past three years.

No wonder they were in demand.

The stallion she'd seen him show the other day was led out. The price rose so quickly she couldn't keep track. It hit over a million. When the bidding halted, she glanced at Nash. He was sipping a soda, his forearms on the rail, totally at ease.

The auctioneer called out the final bid and Hayley gasped. Nash nodded to the auctioneer and the gavel slammed down.

She sagged against the fence. "Amazing."

Nash shrugged. "Seems fair."

"Fair?"

"That's the son of the last Derby winner." He nodded to the horse and its new owner.

"Oh."

"A good two-year-old. I have the foal." He led her away from the pens.

"Was that the one I saw you have put back in the barn the other day?" she asked.

He nodded. "The mare is excellent stock, and her foals will be the eye catchers in two years."

"Do you artificially inseminate?"

He quirked a smile. "Yeah. I'd let them go natural if the stallions didn't get so hot and bothered they hurt the mares."

Hayley reddened.

"For a doctor, you sure do blush a lot."

She elbowed him playfully and he chuckled, finishing off his soda and tossing the can in the trash.

Jimmy Lee rushed up to him, handing him papers to sign, and he chatted with Hayley as Nash read and signed the documents. No sooner had Jimmy left than Andy Pike pushed his way over, followed by three men. The men all shook hands and Andy started in with questions Hayley couldn't begin to understand. Nash stood back a bit, his arms folded over his chest, and she was fascinated with watching him. He had the men's respect, answering questions of breeding methods, veterinary services and cutting techniques. She learned that some of these horses actually went to ranches as far away as Nebraska and Oklahoma. And she also learned that women noticed him, tried waving to get his attention. He'd nod and politely respond with a smile, but the looks they gave him, looks no other woman could mistake for anything but "I want you and I'm available," didn't have much effect. Regardless, she had the urge to step closer.

Finally Nash excused himself and took her arm. "Sorry. Ready to split?"

"Yes," she said with feeling. "My feet are killing me."

They walked to his truck and Nash had to help her into the cab, it was so high off the ground. Leaving the parking lot, she sank into the soft cushions, her hat on her lap. In seconds she was dozing.

Nash glanced at her, thinking the woman was a cross between a fairy in his dreams and a thorn in his side. Despite the distance separating them across the truck cab, he could sense every inch of her like sunshine on his skin, like an animal senses its mate. It was the sweetest torment, like discovering her all over again. Her body was shapelier, and the way she carried herself was as sexy as her walk. And when he kissed her, it was as he'd been gone on a long journey and finally made it home. His fingers flexed on the steering wheel and he looked straight ahead. How was he going to spend the night alone in his house with her and not want to take her to his bed? He groaned, shaking his head. He was going to come apart at the seams if he wasn't careful.

Half an hour later, he pulled into the driveway and shut off the engine. Within minutes they were through the front door. Hayley went around the house flipping on lights, while Nash went to the French doors, peering out onto the patio.

"I'm going to shower and change," he told her, crossing to her.

"Me, too."

"Meet you here."

She nodded, a sudden wave of excitement coursing through her. She knew it wasn't wise to want time alone with him this badly, but she did. She pushed aside the fact that she was leaving, that they were from too-different worlds, and hurried through her shower, pulling on shorts and a T-shirt and not even bothering to dry her hair.

She found him sitting on the back veranda. She stepped out onto the patio, her eyes widening at the meal laid out. Candles, chilling wine and heavenly smelling food under those silver domes. "If you tell me you whipped this up, I quit, and you can take over the cooking."

He stood, pulling out a chair for her. "Not a chance. It's catered."

Her brows rose. "My, my."

"I figured you needed the break and I'm starved." Besides, he thought, he didn't want her to feel as if she had to cook, and the last thing he wanted was her attention diverted.

She slid into the chair, sighing deeply. She tipped her head back, staring at the stars as he poured her a glass of wine. "It's almost sinful doing this."

He eyed her. "You aren't going to refuse, are you?"

She shook her head as he pressed the goblet in her hand. "Of course not. I was going to suggest takeout or delivery."

"When was the last time you pampered yourself?"

Her forehead knitted.

"Can't remember, can you?" His expression was a little too assured for her liking. "Don't you think its about time?"

"I never had the money or the time, Nash, you know it."

He inched his chair closer, uncovering the meal. "I know, darlin', but for the next couple of days, just think of nothing but relaxing." *And being with me,* he thought.

She straightened in the chair, the aroma of food mak-

ing her mouth water. "Sounds like a plan, and you
don't have to tell me twice." She forked a bite of veal.
"This was really sweet of you."

"I didn't do it to be sweet."

She glanced up, the bite halfway to her mouth. "Are
you trying to seduce me, Mr. Rayburn?"

His lips quirked. "Would it work?"

She smiled slightly. "Boy, is that a loaded question."
She ate.

"Don't answer then, just let me dream."

His low tone made her skin go warm, the heat of it
offering memories and a promise of more. She met his
gaze. The air between them simmered with suppressed
sexuality, melting away the barriers he'd struggled to
erase all day. They dined and sipped wine, discussed
politics, the twins, the ranch. They got into a heated
debate over fertility and cloning, and Nash finally had
to concede to her views. She was fighter, battling for
the human race, and he was only seeing the way to
breed a faster stronger horse.

God, he loved her mind.

And he wanted to love her body.

Relaxing in his chair, he couldn't take his gaze off
her. The breeze lifted her red curls. She looked sated,
her eyes closed, a small curiously private smile curving
her lips. He squashed his need to pull her onto his lap
and just shifted closer, facing her, then bent down to
lift her feet onto his lap. She spared him a glance. He
pulled off her sandals and massaged her feet. She
moaned, going limp.

"Come with me," he said.

"Where?"

"For a ride."

She opened one eye.

"On my horse. What a trashy mind."

He provoked it, she thought. "Isn't it dangerous at night?"

"The moon is full and I know this land like I know my own hand."

"Go get your beast, Rayburn. I'll wait here."

He stood. "You aren't going to fall asleep on me, are you?"

"Just getting my second wind, honest." She waved, sinking into the chair.

Nash left and Hayley sighed. *Relax. Enjoy it,* she told herself. *You'll soon be gone, and like everything else, you'll regret it if you don't.* A few minutes later her ears pricked to the sound of hooves. She watched as he rode the horse across the patio, the sight somehow incredibly romantic. She stood up when he stopped in front of her, holding out his hand.

"There's no saddle," she said.

"Just put your foot on top of mine." He flicked his fingers. "I'll do the rest."

She grasped his hand, looking skeptical.

"Trust me, Hayley." Her gaze locked with his. "I won't let anything hurt you."

The words were soft, his look tender and holding more meaning than she wanted to see. *Oh this is dangerous,* she thought and put her foot atop his. He hauled her up before him.

"This is cool," she said with a glance back.

"It gets better."

He urged the horse into a canter, and they raced across the hill, heading for the line of trees a hundred yards away. Hayley laughed, and he gripped her tightly, leaning over the horse's neck with her. The moon shone brightly, turning everything silver, and as he headed into the trees, she tensed.

"It's okay," he said close to her ear. "Trust me."

Her body relaxed with each step and she sagged back against him as he maneuvered the horse through the forest. *There must be a path,* she thought, but she couldn't see one in the dark. Just when she thought the trees would shut out the moonlight completely, the beams speared through the branches, coloring the ground.

Then she saw it. A cove, the river spilling to the tidal basin in a soft rush. Water trickled over rocks and into the marshy pool.

"It's beautiful. Can you swim in it?"

"Yes, but I wouldn't right now."

She glanced back at him questioningly.

"Snakes. Water moccasins. Can't see them in the dark," Nash said.

He chuckled when she lifted her legs, afraid. Then he pulled her warmly against him. He rested his chin on the top of her head, the feel of her in his arms like a dream he'd wished on too many times.

"I used to come here alone."

He didn't have to say while he was married to Michelle. She heard it in his tone.

"I'd sit over there—" he pointed to a cluster of rocks and fallen trees "—and just think and wonder."

"Wonder?"

"About you. About where you were. About what I'd done."

She bowed her head. "Don't."

"Shh. I'd think about some other man touching you, and I'd drive myself mad. I had to remind myself that I'd made my bed and had to lie in it without you. But still, I'd remember what it was like to make love to you, the smell of your skin, the taste of it.''

"Nash." She twisted in his arms, gazing into his tortured eyes.

"I have a very good memory. But it wasn't perfect."

Hers was, with a clarity that bit into her soul. This fight in her, the internal battle she'd waged between longing, the true feelings in her heart and what she should do to survive came to a crushing end at his next words.

"Hayley, I want you. I have for more years than I care to count." His lips brushed hers, his entire body locking tight with a fierce need to have her, to be inside her and hear all those passion-laced cries that haunted his dreams.

"So much for being friends, I see," she said, the words whispering over his lips.

Something inside him broke free and soared. "We were always more than friends."

"Nash."

He inhaled her scent, wanting it spread all over him. "Uh-uh?"

"If you're going to kiss me, then you ought to get to it."

Instantly his mouth covered hers in a lush kiss that fired his already seething blood. Hayley shifted sideways on his lap and arched into him, her skin throbbing for his touch, her breasts filling the space between them. He crushed her to his chest and made love to her mouth with a ferocity that made her want him more.

Denial never entered her mind. There wasn't room. His touch created a warm haze and sent hot sensations, overflowing, crowding her thinking and making her body answer. Suddenly she couldn't get close enough.

A kiss wasn't enough. She shifted her legs and wrapped them around his hips.

Nash groaned darkly. "You're driving me crazy," he whispered into her mouth.

She couldn't help it. Like before when Nash touched her, she didn't have much control.

And right now she didn't care.

Eight

The horse sensed their passion, sidestepping, and the motion pushed them apart.

He held her gaze, his breathing rushed. "This isn't the place for this."

"Depends on your point of view," she said breathlessly, and tightened her legs around him. It ground her softness to the hard length of him straining against his jeans.

"Oh, honey." His hands mapped a wild ride over her bare thighs straddling his and he kissed her again. Before he got carried away and could do nothing about it, he drew back, nipping at her jaw, then the slender line of her throat. "Let's go home."

She smiled, settled her arms around his neck and said, "Fine, go."

He looked down, then met her gaze. "That's not going to be as comfortable a ride as you think."

"Again, I believe that depends on your point of view."

Smiling and shaking his head, he reined the horse around. They both saw the danger in this game. The slow rock of the animal was maddening, grinding their aroused bodies in a familiar dance and drawing up more sensation. Of slick skin, the touch of his mouth where no other had tasted. Of his hardness pushing into her, the delicious friction that drove her mad and made her aware of her insatiable need for more of him. Hayley wanted to taste and touch him. She felt truly a woman in his arms, desired and adored, and the years alone fell away to the moments in the darkness, the scent of this man swirling around her.

Her hand slipped between them, her fingertips shaping him.

Nash couldn't stand it and stopped halfway across the field and kissed her hard, his hands sliding up her back and around to cup her breasts. She moaned, a harsh greedy sound, and she arched into his touch, then pulled at his shirt, freeing it from his waistband. She drove her palms over his warm skin. Nash trembled and threw his head back.

She flicked open the shirt buttons and then her mouth was on him. "Hayley, oh, you're walking a dangerous line."

"I'm trying to destroy your incredible restraint."

He cupped her face, gazing into her eyes. "I've been marshaling it whenever you're around."

"I know. Let's just face it, Nash. No matter what happens between us, in this—" she wiggled and loved that he shuddered and closed his eyes "—we were good together."

He stared for a moment longer, then without a word,

strong hands gripped her waist, and he maneuvered her to face forward.

"Well, this is no fun."

"Wanna bet?"

He cupped her breasts, loving it when she moaned and covered his hands. It only made him want to touch more of her. Right now. And as the horse headed toward the house, Nash slid his hand downward, beneath the band of her shorts. The muscles of her stomach contracted, her hips shifting in open invitation.

"I need to touch you," he said in a frantic tone. "I need to." Hurriedly, he flipped open the button of her shorts, peeled down the zipper and drove his hand beneath the layers of fabric.

He found her, wet and warm, and she cried out in pleasure.

"See what fun this is?"

She laughed shakily, then he drove the breath from her lungs when he parted her and plunged two fingers inside.

"Nash," she chanted, her knees drawing up in response. She laid her head back on his shoulder and reached up to push her fingers into his hair.

He tasted anything he could reach, her mouth, her throat, his words hot in her ear. "Do you know how long I've waited to touch you?" He didn't expect an answer. He felt her tighten and tense with the rush of her desire, and he stopped the horse on the edge of the patio and stroked her into heaven, absorbing her shudders, hearing her short gasps for air. He spoke to her, heightening every sensation careering through her body, telling her how moments like this haunted him, how much he'd longed to be with her, naked and putting his mouth where his fingers were. She cried out, covering

his hand and pulsing on the threshold of glorious pleasure before she sank limply against him.

He held her, wrapping his arms around her waist.

"Hayley, baby, I—"

She silenced him with a kiss, curling into him like a
contented kitten. She didn't want words to break the
spell, but then it was broken by the ringing of the phone
in the house. His face tucked close to hers, he tipped
his wrist to see the time on his watch.

"Who could that be at this hour?"

Hayley instantly pushed his arms away and slid from
the horse. "This late, it can't be good."

Running across the pool deck, she yanked open the
French doors and dashed to the phone. "River Willow."

"Hayley, it's Grace. Thank God I finally reached
you. Kim's hurt and she's hysterical. I can't calm her."

Hayley questioned Grace, and when Nash stepped inside, she held her hand out to him. He came to her.
"Apply pressure and we'll be there as soon as we can."

She handed Nash the phone, then dashed to her room.
She washed and changed into a pair of jeans, then
grabbed her small red duffel bag. She was jamming her
feet into her sneakers when Nash met her in the front
foyer.

"How long will it take?" she said as they trotted
down the front steps.

"Ten minutes if I speed." He helped her in on his
side of the truck and climbed up after her.

"Then speed," she said as he started the engine.
"Your mother didn't tell me how bad it was."

Nash paled and Hayley reached out, rubbing his
shoulder as he tore down the drive to the highway.

* * *

They walked in without knocking, calling for Grace.

Hayley could hear Kim's sobs and panicky shrieks. They followed the sound and Grace rushed out of the spare-bedroom door.

Nash went around the left side of the bed, talking to Kim, but nothing seemed to help. Her mouth and chin were bloody and even he couldn't comfort her.

"It's not that bad and I've tried everything," Grace said in a low voice, the two women out in the hall. "But the sight of her own blood keeps scaring her."

Hayley gripped Grace's shoulders and held her gaze with her own. "Go make some decaf and take Kate with you. I'll take care of this, Grace. Okay?"

Grace nodded and called to Kate. Hayley kissed Kate's head, then moved to Kim on the bed.

"Hey there," she said, sitting down on the side of the bed. "See? One day out of my sight and look what trouble you get into." Hayley smiled and Kim's crying faded to sniffles and pitiful whimpers. Hayley blotted her eyes with a tissue, lovingly pushing her damp hair of her forehead. "You're going to be fine, baby, I promise."

Kim calmed and let out a long tired breath.

Hayley reached for a cloth, inspecting the wound. "Nash, I need cool water, a bowl and more light." He nodded and stood, flicking on the overhead light as he left.

"Well, how did you do this?" Hayley said, unzipping her duffel and pulling out packs of gauze. She tore open the packages, then poured antiseptic on the squares.

"I fell."

"This late?" She blotted the wound. "What were you doing up?"

"I had to go to the bathroom and I couldn't see in the dark."

She put pressure on the child's chin. "Bet you wish you'd turned on the hall lights now, huh?"

Kim nodded, cracking a reluctant smile.

Hayley smiled back and with her free hand cradled Kim's. "So you tripped and hit your chin on the floor?"

She shook her head. "On the edge of the counter."

"Open your mouth." Kim obeyed, and with a penlight Hayley examined her mouth. "You bit your tongue. Just a little," she assured her. "But places like ears and tongues and your head bleed a lot more than other places."

Nash came into the room, setting the cloth and a bowl on the nightstand, then moved to the opposite side of the bed to watch.

"Has she had a tetanus shot?" Hayley asked him.

Nash's brows drew down. "No."

"Hold this." She instructed him to keep pressure on Kim's chin, and as she rummaged in her bag, he talked soothingly to his daughter. Hayley prepared the syringe.

"I have to give you a shot, Kim."

Her eyes growing wide, the child immediately started to squirm.

"This'll keep that from getting infected. Right, Nash?"

"Sure will," he said. Kim looked at her daddy. "I dare any germs to get on my little girl."

Kim smiled before her gaze swung back to Hayley's, then to the syringe. Hayley was already pulling it out of her arm.

"That didn't even hurt!" Kim said, amazed.

"Why, thank you, Miss Kim. You're very brave." Hayley winked and tended the wound. "It needs stitches, at least two." She glanced at Nash, then back to Kim. "I can do it, honey, or we can take you to a hospital and have a doctor there do it."

Kim looked at her dad, her lip quivering with fear, then brought her gaze to Hayley. She touched her hand and in very adult manner said, "I want you to do it. I know you won't hurt me."

Kim's trust was like a banner wrapping around her soul, and Hayley's heart filled with love for the little girl. She patted her hand and looked at Nash. He was now leaning against the wall, his arms folded over his chest.

"I'd trust you with my daughters' lives, Hayley. Go ahead."

She nodded, a lump swelling in her throat. Funny how a couple of stitches were so monumental, she thought, and went about numbing the area with a cream novocaine. She didn't think Kim could take another shot right now. She made the little girl close her eyes, then took two quick stitches and sealed the wound. The one on her tongue would close by morning.

As she worked, Nash studied Hayley, her moves efficient, and he recalled how Michelle used to fall apart over the littlest crisis. She was never this independent and self-assured, and at first, he'd felt flattered to be needed. But with his children, Michelle was helpless. Watching Hayley calm his mother and his daughters, he realized he wanted a woman who was less dependent on him. He wanted Hayley.

Kim smiled. "I can't feel nothing."

"Anything," both Nash and Hayley corrected at once, then laughed.

"Your tongue is going to hurt a little later on, but it will heal fast. I want you to rinse your mouth with salt-water in the morning. Okay?"

When Hayley finished applying a small bandage to her chin, she kissed Kim. And the girl hugged her tightly. Hayley closed her eyes, savoring the feel of the little arms around her neck and tears burned. *Oh, I will miss them,* she thought. "I think we could use a treat about now," Hayley said. "A Popsicle for that tongue." Kim's face lit up. "Come on. Let's go see what Grandma Grace has in that big ol' kitchen." Hayley stood, holding out the child's robe, and Kim climbed off the bed and pushed her arms into the sleeves.

"Thank you, Miss Hayley."

"You're welcome, honey." Taking her hand, they left together.

Nash was slower to follow, glancing at the duffel bag and the small plastic bag Hayley had put her used materials in. He collected her things and the bowl of water, then carried them to the kitchen. The girls sat at the table, sucking Popsicles. Kim looked funny as she tried to suck the Popsicle and hold an ice pack to her chin at the same time. His mom was leaning against the counter, cupping a mug of coffee. Hayley took her things from Nash, put the bowl in the dishwasher, then offered him some coffee.

"Thanks so much, Hayley," Grace said softly. "I don't know what I'd have done."

"You'd have taken her to the hospital, Grace."

"But the hysterics. I don't remember Samantha being like that."

"That's because she was a tomboy," Nash said, sipping his coffee.

Grace looked adoringly at her granddaughters. "Yes, I suppose you're right."

"We don't have to go home, do we, Daddy?" Kate looked at her sister almost accusingly.

"I don't think that will be necessary," Grace said. "Besides, we can still do what we'd planned." Grace winked at the girls and they grinned.

"Mom," Nash said, a hit of suspicion in his voice.

"Oh, Nash, we'll be fine, now that Hayley came to the rescue."

"I brought her," he said in his defense.

"Oh, big man," his mother said, winking at Hayley. "We're going to have a girls' day—lunch, shopping, get our hair done, you know."

"No, he doesn't, but I do." Hayley grinned at Nash. "I feel outnumbered."

"On a plantation with twenty men, how do you think *we* feel?" Hayley said, and Nash liked the "we" part of that statement.

After the Popsicles and a pain reliever for Kim, Nash and Hayley tucked them into bed. At the front door Grace hugged Hayley.

"Thank you, sweetie."

"You're welcome," Hayley said, savoring the motherly hug. It had been a long time since she'd felt this close to another woman.

"Are you sure you want to keep them?"

"Oh, of course. I know how busy Nash gets around this time of year. Y'all go off and have some fun," Grace said.

Hayley caught the matchmaking hint in her voice, but decided to ignore it. "I'll need to remove the stitches in a couple of days. And give this to her if she's in pain." She handed her a small bottle of children's aspirin. "Kim's chin is going to throb, so she'll need an ice pack on it till she falls asleep, then one in the morning, to keep down the swelling."

Grace nodded and walked with them onto the porch. Nash and Hayley were driving down the road when he said, "You know more about family than you think."

She looked at him. "Doctoring a wound has nothing to do with family."

His fingers flexed on the steering wheel. "You're not giving it a chance."

"I don't have the time to give anything a chance. We've been over this before."

"No, you have in your mind, but you haven't talked to me about it."

"What's there to say? Residency takes up a lot of hours, and you and the girls deserve better."

"I would never ask you to delay your career, honey."

"You did once."

He sighed, turning into his drive. "We've come full circle, haven't we?"

"I guess so."

"You know that even before Michelle interfered, I wanted to marry you."

Her breath hitched. "I know. But you wanted a wife and mother when I didn't know a thing about being either."

"And you think I knew how to be a husband and father? It's an experience learned over time."

"I know, but I've never had what you've had."

"Who says you can't have it now?" In the driveway, he stopped the truck in front of the house, then shut off the engine and faced her. "I could have helped you through your schooling, at least taken some of the burden. I never wanted you to give up your dream."

"It's water under the bridge. Your *duty* to Michelle sort of makes this conversation null and void, doesn't it? We never got the chance to work anything out, and we can't now." It hurt even to think of what she would have to give up.

"Dammit, Hayley, do you have to be so stubborn?"

"What do you want from me?"

"Everything," he said selfishly. "And I want to give that to you. too."

"Well, I owe a hospital my time and attention. I'll be practically living there. That's not fair to you." She opened the door and climbed down.

And Nash was there, gripping her arms. "Are you telling me to go find someone else?"

Her heart nearly shattered at the thought. "Do whatever you have to."

He would, he decided right then. If he had to fight harder for her, he would pull out all the stops. And he started with a kiss, his mouth a hard slash across hers. She clung to him, devouring, and silencing the fight. He put everything he had into the single kiss, mastering her mouth, pushing his body into hers, then just as suddenly he pulled back.

"*Now* tell me to go find someone else."

She sputtered but didn't say anything, her head and body reeling.

"I want you. No other will do, Hayley. No other ever has."

He turned her around and faced her toward the house, giving her a push when she didn't move. She didn't respond to his high-handed measures. She couldn't. Her body went nuclear after that kiss, and she was having difficulty getting back her control. When he escorted her like a child to her bedroom door, he stopped and looked down at her.

"I have appointments in the morning and won't be back till five at the earliest. There's an auctioneers' dance and we're going."

Her hands on her hips, she glared up at him. "Excuse me?"

"I won't take no for an answer, Hayley. Be ready by seven."

He took a few steps away, then stopped when she called, "I hate bullies and this doesn't change a damn thing and...and...I don't have a thing to wear to a dance."

He eyed her from her sneakers to the top of her head. "That's a lame excuse. You just be ready."

"See if I will, Nash Rayburn!" She went into her room and slammed the door.

Nash sighed hard and rubbed his hand over his face. He hated making demands on her, but why was she so dead set against even giving them a chance? Why didn't she see that they could work this out if she'd just co-operate a little. He blamed her father for this, sending a child off to take care of herself. She'd done it for so long, looking out for herself alone, she didn't know how to let anyone else in. As she had when they were to-gether before, she was terrified that if she let anyone into her life so completely, she'd lose it all again. And he knew it was harder for her, because he was the one person she'd let get close, and he'd betrayed that trust. She was too independent and didn't want to be anyone's responsibility, let alone share her burdens with him. And he wanted to share them. He just had to make her understand that. And if she denied them this chance, Nash knew he'd never recover.

* * *

Hayley was furious most of the day, stewing over his arrogant demands. Just who did he think he was, telling her they were going out to a dance without asking her first? She vented her anger by cleaning house and washing clothes. She weeded the flower beds around the house although a gardener came twice a month to do it.

She was alone on the plantation, and for a while she strolled the grounds, walked through the barns and chatted with the horses. She even swept and cleaned up in there. Sweating and dirty, she considered staying just like that when he returned. It would serve him right to go to this dance alone. Yet, regardless, she was in her room, thumbing through her clothes hanging in the closet, trying to find something suitable, when the doorbell rang. Sighing irritatedly, she pitied the fool on the other side of the door as she flung it open.

A woman, dark-haired and smartly dressed, stood on the porch.

"Dr. Albright?"

"Yes."

"I'm Mary Faith Rockwell. I own the shop on Sycamore, the Blue Swan."

Hayley smiled. "Oh, I saw that shop. You have some lovely things in the window."

"Thank you. You must stop in sometime. I've got a few garments that would look spectacular on you."

Hayley wasn't going to mention that she couldn't afford her prices. "What are you doing here? Nash is gone till—"

"Oh, I know." She stepped back out of sight for a moment, then came back with a white plastic garment bag, emblazoned with her shop's logo, a blue swan. "This is for you." She pressed it into her hands. "And this.'' She added a large hatbox. ''Enjoy,'' she said, and turned on her heel, moving quickly down the porch to her car.

''I didn't buy anything,'' Hayley called out.

''There's a card inside the box,'' the woman said with a private smile as she slipped into her car.

Hayley stared at the package, then at Mary Faith driving away. Closing the door, she went immediately to her room, set the hatbox down and pulled the garment from the bag.

A filmy sage-green chiffon duster lay like a spider web over a silk-beaded sheath dress in the same color. The jacket was long, sheer and crisp. It looked like a cloud wrapping the dress. Hayley loved it. She'd never seen anything so elegant. Quickly she opened the hatbox. Inside was a matching clutch and skimpy delicate heeled sandals. There were stockings and even a bra and a pair of the tiniest sage-green panties inside. Then she saw the card, recognizing Nash's handwriting.

She opened the tiny envelope and read: *Come be my belle of the ball.*

Hayley sank onto the bed, her eyes burning with tears. Well, dang. How was she supposed to stay mad at him now? She admitted she'd heard of the dance while at the rodeo and had been wondering if he'd attend. She still wanted to smack him for being such a bully last night. He had to learn he couldn't get his way just because he was a man. She looked at the outfit. It was gorgeous, and the elegance of it told her this wasn't just a country dance.

She battled with her pride for about two seconds, then hung the dress on the back of the door and dashed to the bathroom to get cleaned up.

* * *

Nash paced the foyer. Hayley didn't answer when he'd knocked on her bedroom door a few minutes ago, and he wondered if she was ever going to come out. At least if she did do it to just holler at him, he'd have a fighting chance.

The sound of her heels on the wood floor brought his head up, and he stopped when the door swung open.

She took his breath away.

The dress fit her like a glove, the chiffon enveloping her in a haze of pale green. And the heeled shoes showed every muscle of her legs in clear definition.

''It's a little short,'' she said, and he dragged his gaze from her legs.

''You're stunning.''

''Thank you.'' She stepped closer. ''Thank you for the outfit.''

He eyed her for a second. ''You aren't going to yell at me for buying it, are you?''

She shook her head and he sighed, relieved. ''You didn't have to bully me, you know.''

He groaned. ''Ah, honey, I know, but when you keep talking about leaving me, I get so fired up.''

''Then let's not talk about it.''

His lips thinned and he forced a smile. ''Agreed. Let's go.''

Outside the sedan was running, and as they walked toward it, she laughed.

Her rubber chicken was firmly ensconced in the grill-work.

Her gaze flew to his. She was deeply touched. ''You're not going to be embarrassed?''

''No, ma'am, and Lurlene is in the garage whenever you want her,'' he said as he held the door for her.

She slipped into the seat and didn't respond until he

was in the car. "Good Lord, Nash, what will you do? They'll all think you've developed a sense of humor."

"I have one."

"Yeah, right. *Now*."

Chuckling, he put the car in gear.

Half an hour later, they pulled up in front of the country club. A valet opened her door, and she glanced at Nash as he handed the man a tip and came to her. He looked good enough to eat, she thought. He was dressed in a black tuxedo, the cut of the jacket boxy and shorter than the normal, and showing off pleated slacks. His white shirt had a band color and he didn't wear a tie, but with his satin vest, low slung and fitted, and that black cowboy hat, he looked more like a gentleman gunslinger than the owner of the oldest plantation in the area. They walked through the doors and handed the hat to a checker.

Music filled the air, and they moved through the wide-open doors into the ballroom.

Heads turned, and Nash smiled privately and proudly to himself. She stopped men in her tracks and she didn't even notice, he thought. She was too busy looking at all the activity. He introduced her around a little, then brought them to their table.

Hayley had never seen anything so beautiful and tried not to gawk. Chandeliers glittered overhead, and the walls and doorways were draped in foamy white tulle and berry-colored flowers. The tables were covered in berry-colored cloths, stark white flowers accenting the vibrant hue. Waiters moved through the clusters, and people danced and dined. China clinked and corks popped. The entire ballroom sparkled like a diamond, and Hayley felt like a princess on Nash's arm.

He smiled down at her.

"Just a little ol' country dance, huh?" she said.

"It gets more elaborate every year. The first time I attended I was a teenager and there was sawdust on the floor."

He didn't give her time to sit, taking her handbag and leaving it at their table before he pulled her onto the dance floor.

"I've wanted to hold you all day."

"Funny. You wanted to brain me yesterday."

"I've seen the error of my ways. Forgive me?"

She cocked her head. "I seem to be doing that a lot lately."

He smiled. He was hoping for years of her forgiveness, since he knew he'd screw up again soon enough.

They danced slowly, Nash pulling her closer with each step. He could feel her shape in the thin dress, her soft form burning through his clothes. His body reacted and his slacks offered little barrier. She felt it, a tiny moan escaping her, but she didn't step back.

"Oh, my, Nashville." She felt empowered by the feel of his groin swelling against her.

He bent to whisper in her ear. "Was there any doubt I wanted you, sprite?" His voice had a husky seductive pitch. "In my life and in my bed."

Nine

Hot sensation rippled through her and she gripped him a little more tightly.

"Nash, stop teasing me," she moaned.

He swung her effortlessly around the dance floor, and close to her ear he whispered, "I mean business, darlin'. And if we weren't in public I'd have you out of that sweet little dress and being shameless with me."

"Please don't talk like that. I can't…it's just that…"

Nash gazed down into her soulful brown eyes and saw her reservations there as much as he heard them in her voice. "You've got to trust somebody sometime, honey. Just be with me, Hayley. Like there is no tomorrow. No," he said when she tried to speak. "I know there is, but let the worries go. Now is all that counts."

Now. Oh, she wanted much more than a few moments with him, and yet she could only nod, the heat in his eyes and the warmth of his touch fogging her mind. The music slowed to a soft samba, and his hips took on a life of their own.

"You're getting nasty," she said when he shifted his hips against her.

"I'm dancing, can't you tell?"

He was being his old seductive self, she thought. She never knew a man who aroused her the way Nash did. He only had to look at her, and her body called out to his. When he touched her, it screamed for him, and worse than fighting her desire for him was remembering what an incredible lover he was.

The music slowed and he brought her deeper into his arms. She was glad he was a good dancer and a great lead, because she'd have fallen all over her feet if he kept staring at her like that. His eyes seemed darker, hotter, and they dragged over her as if they had the power of touch. Her breath quickened. Oh, how she wished they were alone right now.

"Everyone's asking about you," he said.

"And what did you say?"

"That you're Dr. Hayley Albright and you're with me."

Somehow she knew he'd said a little more than that, and her heart did a quick dive and hop. "Nash." Her hand slid to the nape of his neck, toying with his hair. He made a soft groaning sound she remembered well, and as he ducked his head, his gaze flicking between her eyes and her mouth, anticipation engulfed her. "This is rather public." Yet she rose up on tiptoe.

"Do it anyway."

Her lips met his and he kissed her softly, holding back the passion that drove through him whenever he was near her, whenever he touched her. She trembled against him, her lips worrying his and he felt her restraint. He reveled in it.

She pulled back, breathless, her eyes glazed. "People are staring."

"We could always take this home." Nash arched a brow, the invitation unmistakable.

Uncertainly swept over her and she knew what he was asking, knew what she wanted. It was a step she wasn't sure she should take. Being so intimate with him last night left her feeling more lost, grasping for that elusive spot that connected her to him again. Making love with him would forge the bond, and she didn't know if she could handle it. Because it would be intense and wild, burning his imprint into her soul. Again.

He danced her into the center of the room, and the music became more seductive, a sultry Latin beat. The feel of his body rocking against hers was electrifying. Their gazes locked and even as he spun her out, then back into his arms, he never broke eye contact. It sent a sensation of unclaimed passion through her, heating her blood, and she responded, their dance growing more seductive, more like foreplay, and the world around them faded.

"What are you thinking?" she asked.

"That I know what's beneath that dress."

She smiled, catlike. "How'd you know they'd fit?"

She was referring mostly to the bra and he grinned. "I just used my hands."

Her brows knitted for a second.

"I figured if those beautiful breasts filled my hands—" she gasped at the image "—then the bra would fit."

"You're shameless sometimes."

He jerked her hard against him, his knee insinuating

between her thighs as he sambaed her around the room. "Just being near you makes me feel wild, darlin'."

She cocked her head. "We did do some outrageous things."

"Things? That's dang polite." He bent to whisper in her ear. "It was hot jungle sex, on my kitchen floor, in the tub, and how about the time we were on those dirt bikes?" A little moan worked in her throat and she closed her eyes briefly. "You looked as good naked and straddling that bike as you did straddling me."

She squeezed him, then after a second, tipped her head to look at him. He saw something in her expression.

"What?" Nash's heart slammed to his stomach. She looked sad all of a sudden.

"That was the last time you touched me. The last time I ever saw you."

Nash stopped and swept her hair off her cheek, then cupped her jaw. "I know. I'm sorry. Baby, you have to know how much I—"

Someone tapped him on the shoulder and they turned to find a waiter standing close. He motioned to the door, and Hayley saw Grace and the girls standing there. "You didn't tell me they'd be stopping by."

"I didn't know," Nash said, and she heard the tinge of irritation in his voice.

Hayley gave him a "be patient" look, then grabbed his hand, pulling him behind her, but after a few steps, she let him go and walked as fast as dignity would allow to the children. She squatted and opened her arms.

"Hi there!" They hugged her tightly. "This is a nice surprise!" With their arms still around her neck, she glanced up at Grace. "Everything okay?"

"Oh, yes, they just wanted to see you and their daddy all dressed up, and I didn't think you'd mind."

"No, of course not."

The girls eased back. "You look *so* pretty, Miss Hayley," Kate said, awe in her voice.

"Thank you, darling. Kind of a change, huh?"

"That's a lovely dress, dear," Grace said.

Her gaze swung briefly to Grace's. "Nash picked it out." Grace's smile grew wide.

Hayley rolled her eyes at the woman and inspected Kim's stitches. "Hurt?"

"No, ma'am, only when I yawn."

Hayley laughed, giving the bandage a kiss, then felt Nash move up behind her.

She stood up and he lifted his girls, one in each arm, and said, "Isn't it past your bedtime?"

They just grinned. "Yup. Waaay past."

"You lost a tooth!" Hayley said to Kate. Nash eyed it very closely and his daughter giggled.

Nash nodded to somewhere behind her. "Hayley? This is Dr. Swanson."

She turned sharply to the old man he'd been talking to earlier. They shook hands, and at her request, he inspected Kate's stitches.

"Fine job, Doctor. Fine."

Hayley thanked him, then asked him if he thought she should have made another stitch. The pair stood off to the side, talking medicine, Nash supposed. When the girls had arrived, there wasn't a person in the room who could mistake her excitement at seeing them. Or at receiving Kim and Kate's crushing hugs. It made him understand again that his daughters were at risk, that their tender hearts could be badly bruised if Hayley suddenly vanished from their lives. A wild stab of pain shot through his chest, and he hefted his daughters a little tighter, accepting their kisses, their hands smoothing his hair; yet his gaze was on Hayley. He wanted a second chance, but at what cost? To him, to her and his girls.

Was trying to convince the woman that he was here for her, that he wanted to work this relationship out when she was hell-bent on going forward alone, asking too much of the other people in his life? If she would give him a clue that she wanted it, too, that she was willing to go the distance, maybe he wouldn't feel as if he was adrift without an oar.

He set the girls down and Grace herded them toward the door.

His heart nearly broke at the way they glanced back over their shoulders at Hayley, but when she looked in their direction, she excused herself from the doctor and went to them.

"Leaving without saying goodbye? Why, I'm stricken, ladies, positively stricken," she said with a deep drawl and a teasing smile. The children hugged and kissed her, and Hayley whispered something private in their ears before they giggled and left with Grace.

Sighing, she waved as they passed through the door, then turned back to Nash. He was looking at her oddly, scowling almost.

"What's wrong?" she asked.

"You love them."

"Yes, very much." She moved nearer, linking her arm with his. He was stiff beside her. "You have a problem with that?"

"They're going to be hurt when you leave."

She stopped and met his gaze. "Would you rather I leave now?"

"I don't want you to go at all."

"Well, that's not an option, and who said to act as if there were no tomorrow?"

"That was before I realized how attached my daughters were to you. They've never responded to anyone like this. And they've never had a mother, not that they can remember."

"Are you blaming me for that?"

Nash sighed and looked away. Dancers moved and people dined in quiet elegance, while he wanted to howl in frustration. "No, of course not, but I have to think of them, too."

"Sure you do. They're your children. Perhaps I should save you the trouble of making that decision."

His gaze snapped back to hers, and the suppressed anger there made her take a step back. "No."

"This is obviously not the place to have a serious discussion." Hayley felt as if the floor was slowly opening beneath her feet, and she feared she could never stop the plunge. Instead, he pulled her onto the dance floor, but the sensual tenderness they'd shared earlier had faded. It stung. When the music ended, he walked her to their table and into her chair like a punished child, then muttered something about getting a drink. Hayley grabbed her purse and headed for the door.

Nash caught her outside the ballroom. "Where are you going?"

"I don't need to be treated like a treasure one minute and an old shoe the next, Nash." She tried to keep the hurt out of her voice and failed. "What is the matter with you?"

"It's that I'm trying hard not to remember you'll leave."

Her look was indignant. "I'm not dying, for pity's

sake. You act like if I walk out the door I'll never look
back. Why is it always black and white to you?''

''Because I want all or nothing.''

She searched his handsome face for a long moment,
swallowing repeatedly. ''Well, you can't have it all.''
Tears filled her eyes. ''So I guess you get nothing.''

His heart squeezed as she yanked free and strode to
the club doors.

Ten

Nash strode after her, unmindful of the people watching as he passed through the country-club doors. He found her hailing a cab.

Quickly he pressed his valet ticket into the attendant's hand and stepped close to her. "Dammit, Hayley. Don't cut me out like this." His voice was low and edged with anger. "It's not all black and white, and we both know it."

She scoffed a dry brittle sound. "It's you who doesn't see that, Nash. You keep drawing lines in the sand, daring me to cross them, and I can't do it."

The cab pulled to a stop. When she made to step toward it, he shut the cab door and waved the driver on.

She glared at him. "You're getting a mighty high-handed—"

"I'm crossing the line." He gripped her arms, pushing his body into hers, the look in his eyes leaving no doubt about his feelings. "No past, no future, only now, Hayley. Right now," he growled. "And I'm done talking."

He kissed her, and in an instant he was deep in her mouth, his tongue thrusting and sweeping. She gave a low moan of want and loneliness and a dark hunger that touched his soul and fueled his desire. The valet pulled the sedan to a stop on the street beside them and still he kissed her. The young man paused to gawk, then moved around the vehicle, leaving the driver's door open. Nash never broke their kiss, running his hands up her spine, and his mouth back and forth over hers. Someone whistled and said his name, and he tore his mouth away, breathing deeply and gazing into her eyes.

"Nash? What's gotten into you?"

"You," he said, and handed her into the passenger seat. His look was long and thorough and completely sexual. Her lips were swollen from his kiss, inviting more, and he was going to take it. Just as soon as they had privacy. He closed the door and walked around the front of the car, tipping the attendant and sliding behind the wheel. He started to say something, then reached across to kiss her again, a hot slide of lips and tongue and utter madness. He set her back into her seat and drove away.

Hayley felt numb with sensual heat. The power of his kiss left her breathless and aroused, and at the first stop sign, he turned to her.

"If you won't come to me, I'll come to you." He kissed her again, nearly dragging her out of her seat and across the console to get her closer to him.

"Who said I wouldn't come to you?"

He chuckled low, and his hand grazed her thigh and

slipped under the hem of her dress, cupping her buttocks as he kissed her and kissed her. She let him, wanted him to touch her again. Last night fused in her mind, bringing untamed desire and erotic heat she hadn't felt in years, hadn't felt with any man but Nash. Oh, how she missed him, missed his power, the way he could turn her inside out and make her love it. He eased back into his seat and stepped on the gas, yet his hand remained on her thigh, fingertips playing over her skin.

"You're enjoying this?" she asked.

He arched a brow. "Aren't you?"

"You're teasing me."

There was a dare in her tone he didn't mistake. "Well, then, I can fix that." He cast her a heavy-lidded glance as his hand slipped between her legs. She licked her lips and let out a long slow breath. It was erotic, his touching her like this, and when he came to a stoplight, he leaned over to kiss her again, his fingertip drawing over the lacy pattern of her panties.

Nash felt a rush of heat and dampness. He cupped her, squeezing gently, and she gasped.

"Oh, mercy!"

His lips worried hers, and he nudged her thighs wider apart, his fingertip edging the band of her panties.

The light changed. He drew back and stepped on the gas, pushing his hand beneath the delicate fabric as the car lurched. She moaned, breathing rapidly, and he kept his eyes on the road as he parted her, sliding his finger into the wet haven.

"Oh, you're so warm and wet." Nash shifted in his seat, his groin heavy with want, and as he eased to a stop at another light, thrust two fingers deep inside her. A truck pulled up beside them.

She tensed. "They'll see."

"Shh," he hushed, and stroked her until she was shuddering and boneless. "The windows are tinted, and do you really care?"

"No— Oh, my!" she gasped. The light changed and he drove. His breathing increased with hers. She let her hand ride over his knee, then upward to shape the hardness straining against his trousers.

"Stop that or we'll have an accident." She cast him a glance, smiling, her body thrusting into his touch, her eyes glowing with desire. He tasted the skin of her throat, the shell of her ear, trying to keep his eyes on the road when the spectacle beside him was so much more interesting.

Hayley moaned, the erotic burn of his touch, of being in the car, in public, made her smile and accept. She cried out when he thrust his fingers inside her with deep intentional strokes. He watched her writhe, adoring her soft pants, her undulating hips, and when he pulled into his driveway, he gunned it to the house, slammed on the brakes and finished what he started.

He let the seat back, pulling her on top of him, her back to his chest as he rubbed and played, his left hand on her breast, and wished she was naked and he was inside her. Her breath hitched, her body tensed, and the sound she made, sexy and familiar, made him harder, made him want to take her now. But he drew her to heaven and refused to stop even as she sank to earth. He opened the door, leaving the car and taking her with him out his side. Then he had her against the cool metal of the car and was leaning against her before she could take a breath. His hunger surged out of proportion; she could feel every inch of it in the fire of his kiss. He pulled her away from the car, his mouth on hers as he back stepped. They parted long enough to make the front steps, yet stopped on the landing to give in to the passion with a thick liquid kiss. In each other's arms, Nash groped for the door.

Shoving it open, he staggered inside and pressed her against the nearest wall.

His mouth was on hers again, hot and fierce.

His fingers wrapped behind one of her knees, lifting her leg and wedging her to his hardness. "Hayley…baby…I want you."

"Do tell," she panted, nibbling his jawline before taking his kiss again.

He chuckled. "What gave me away?"

"This." She thrust her hips forward, his arousal mashing against her.

In the foyer, any hesitation fled like refracting light as her heel touched the wood floor. His jacket fell, then shirt studs scattered like tacks as she advanced on him, stripping him. Fine white linen fluttered to the floor. Her sheer overdress joined it, then her hand was inside his trousers, enfolding him, stroking him, and he moaned, throwing his head back and letting her play.

He couldn't take it, his body throbbing, and when he caught their reflection in the mirror suspended above the credenza, he turned her toward it, pressing his lips to the nape of her neck, telling her how good she smelled, that he could almost taste her heat. Her skin glistened softly and he licked it as he unzipped her dress, then unfastened her bra. Impatiently he slipped his hands inside to envelop her breasts.

A moan of satisfaction escaped into the stillness. She pushed back into him.

"Oh, Nash. I've missed you." Hayley covered his hands, then let the sage-green dress and bra fall to her ankles. He devoured the curve of her spine, the bend of her hip. She stood before him in a satin thong panty and high heels. Nash thought he'd die just looking at her, and he hooked his thumbs in the thin panty straps and peeled them down.

She shuddered and gripped the polished ledge, her body yearning for the heat of him. He disappeared from view in the mirror, but she could feel him kissing her buttocks, stroking the inside of her thighs. His mouth was everywhere, and stepping out of the garment barely registered.

He stood, running his hands up her sides, and she twisted to face him.

She was on him, pushing his trousers down, and he sank to his knees, taking her with him. She straddled him, wet heat sliding over his hardness, pulsing to be filled, and he groaned, a dark lusty sound of pure male pleasure. He gripped her hips. She circled him, in control now, brushing his arousal across her damp treasure.

Nash shuddered, gazing into her eyes. "Honey, we need protection."

"I have it covered," she said as she rose up slightly.

Her gaze locked with his. He entered her, and a quick staggered breath passed her parted lips.

Tears wet her eyes, and she held his face in her hands and sank down onto him. Nash closed his eyes and felt her feminine flesh grip him in a tight fist of pleasure.

"Hayley."

"Mercy, did you grow?" she gasped.

He smiled, his gaze a prisoner of hers. Gripping his shoulders, she surged closer, taking him fully into herself. She could not be contained. Not that he would try. She was glorious, uninhibited, and Nash felt the blood barrel through his veins as she cried out, laughing. Then he pushed her onto her back and braced himself above her.

He withdrew and plunged, over and over, each thrust driving her across the floor. She accepted it, willed him to unleash himself on her, her hips rising to greet his. He quickened and her fingertips dug into his chest. She pulsed and flexed, arching, calling his name as he slammed into her.

His primal groan vibrated through the house. His body quaked with bone-racking tremors. Heat spilled and they stared, suspended, as raw pleasure peaked through them. Her lips parted, a shuddering breath tumbled free, and he drank in the taste, grinding into her till the last of her passion perished.

Spent, she sagged to the floor. He lowered himself slowly onto her, kissing her mouth, her brow, her closed eyes.

Her lashes swept up. And Hayley knew in that instant she'd already fallen in love with him again. It was a battle she'd tried fighting, but lost the instant he'd first touched her.

"We're better with age," he said, and she touched his lips. He caught one fingertip between his teeth.

"Yeah." Her smile was slight. Oh, the things he showed only her, she thought.

"I'd like to stay right like this," he said, easing back.

She went with him, wrapping her arms around his neck. "I love it when you misbehave."

"And you're just so hard to coax, huh?" He grinned and glanced around. Clothes lay in rumpled heaps around them. He picked up her satin panties, winging them on his fingertip. She gave him a playful shove, then shifted off his lap.

Nash flinched, the separation almost painful. He

gazed up at her as she stood, her bare breasts jiggling in his face.

"Come on, cowboy. We aren't done yet." She turned and walked toward his bedroom.

For a second Nash couldn't move, entranced as he watched her go, deliciously naked except for a delicate pair of high heels.

She was the hottest creature on the planet, he decided, and struggled to his feet. He considered gathering up their clothes, then just hitched up his trousers, and followed her.

She was right. They weren't done. And this time he'd make slow luscious love to her, in his ancestor's bed, where they belonged.

Hayley sat on the far corner of the huge four-poster bed, watching Nash sleep.

She loved him. She known it all along and couldn't say whether or not she ever fell out of love with him, but this time it was different. This time she loved him with her soul and knew no matter what occurred, she'd still love him. And she hated that she had to leave. But she knew that if residency was anything like her internship, then her days would be filled with long hours, little sleep and studying. People might call her Doctor, but she wasn't there yet, though she'd had more training than most at this point in her career. It hadn't even taken off yet, she thought. She didn't know if she could handle more complications in her life.

But she wanted Nash, and if this was all she'd get for now, then she'd savor every moment. He stirred and rolled over, flinging his arm above his head, and her gaze drifted over his body, bare but for the sheet pooled at his waist. He was an incredible specimen of man, she thought, his wide shoulders nearly covering the pillow. His stomach was tight and flat, a sleek six-pack of rippling muscles itching to be touched.

She shifted, her body gloriously tender from the past few hours, then eased across the bed and down beside him.

"I knew you were still here." His arm wrapped around her, his hand riding the curve of her hip.

"There's only right now."

He opened his eyes, his gaze searching hers.

"I love you," she said.

He simply stared back, his hand trembling a bit as he turned to face her and brushed the hair from her temple. "I'm in love with you, too."

Her lips curved gently. His claim spread over her like a warm blanket. "I was hoping for that."

"I never fell out of love with you."

Her eyes burned, and Hayley knew there was no other place for her to be than right here. She pushed him onto his back, half over him, and kissed him softly, a play of lips, a swipe of her tongue, and she rejoiced in his trembling.

Then her tongue snaked over his nipple and Nash let out a low growl.

Hayley laughed and slid her hand down his taut stomach and under the sheets. She found him, warm and hard.

"What are you doing, woman?"

She grinned and ducked under the covers. He arched and swore, then sank into the mattress as her mouth took possession.

"Want more?" she asked.

His hands fisted. "Yes, ahh…no…good grief!"

"Lost for words, darling?"

"Lost is more like it." He tossed back the covers.

She smiled, catlike, and took him into her mouth again, a devilish gleam in her eyes.

Nash couldn't take it, and he grabbed her, flipping her on the bed facedown. "You'll pay dearly."

"So you say."

His hands mapped her from thighs to throat, and he levered her to her knees, wrapping her fingers over the carved headboard. Then, his knees between hers, he slid into her, wild heat surrounding him. "I get harder just being inside you," he whispered, shaping her breasts, toying with her nipples.

"I know, I feel it." She pushed away, then eased back.

Nash took complete possession, their position offering him a playground of womanly softness. He plunged into her and plunged his hand between her spread thighs, loving her cries and gasps, the way she bucked and called his name in a long moan.

He told her how beautiful she was, that he'd never made love in this bed with any woman, and the impact of his words made her still for a second and look back over her shoulder at him. A sheen glazed her eyes and again they christened the two-hundred-year-old bed. The grand timbers shook as he thrust, loving her in smooth cadence fused with friction, and when she begged for more as if she couldn't get enough of him, he held her tightly and spilled his seed into her, wishing it would take root and bind her to him. She bowed beautifully, her head flung back, as her pleasure exploded, making him drunk for more.

They collapsed on the bed, and she curled into his

AMY J. FETZER   155

strength, his arms wrapped around her. His lips on her throat, Nash didn't want the sun to rise, didn't want the world to interfere. He wanted only Hayley and any time he could have with her.

Eleven

Hayley reached for the ringing phone and mumbled hello and the name of the plantation.

"Hayley, dear, this is Grace."

Sleepily, she rolled over, rubbing her face. The sound of the shower running came to her as she glanced at the alarm clock. The early hour made her sit up sharply. "Are the girls all right?"

"Fine, just fine. I'm calling to ask Nash if they can stay over an extra day or two. My neighbor's grandchildren are coming in for a visit, and since they know the twins, they'd have a good time."

How nice it must be for the girls to have so many friends, Hayley thought.

"Is he around?"

"Just a sec." Hayley left the bed, pulling the tangled sheet with her, and opened the bathroom door with the phone still tucked against her ear.

"Is that the shower?" Grace asked.

"Yes."

"Hayley…" There was a bit of hesitancy in Grace's voice that should have alerted her. "Are you in his bedroom?"

Hayley stilled, realizing her blunder. "Well, ah, yes. I am." There was no way around this, and Hayley wasn't the least bit embarrassed about sharing herself with Nash.

"Thank God."

"Grace!" Hayley sputtered.

"Honey, if you can't see that you two were meant for each other, then maybe a little hot sex will help."

Hayley burst with laughter. She adored this woman. "I won't even go there, Grace Rayburn."

Nash poked his head out the shower door, frowning, his gaze flicking to the phone.

Hayley held it out to him. "Your mother." Then she said into the phone just before she handed it over, "Who is being a shameless tart."

She started to walk away, but Nash snagged the sheet and hauled her back. He dripped water all over her as he put the phone to his ear.

"Yes, they can. No, we're staying right here." He wiggled his eyebrows and bent to kiss Hayley's mouth. "Yes, Mom, I do love her."

Hayley breath caught, and she touched his cheek. "I love you, too," she whispered.

"Oh, I plan to," he said with a long look down her body as he drew the sheet aside. He tipped the phone away from his mouth. "When do the stitches need to come out?" he said to her.

She grappled with the sheet as if Grace could see them. "Tomorrow is okay."

"All right if mom's doctor takes them out?" She nodded and into the phone he said, "Yes, that's fine. See you in a few days. Bye." He clicked off the phone and tossed it on a pile of towels, then with a grin, pulled her into the steamy shower with him.

He kissed her, the spray hot and strong and awakening her body.

"Good morning," he murmured against her lips, then picked up the soap, lathering her breasts and massaging them in slow wet circles.

Hayley gripped his hips, wondering how they had the energy for this, then finding it as his lips closed over her nipple. He drew on it deeply, humming as if tasting a light confection, his tongue rasping over the sensitive tips again and again until Hayley thought she'd melt into the tile floor.

Then he knelt on one knee, soaping her thighs, her buttocks, and murmured something about loving her awake for the rest of her life. A little tinge of sadness pulled through her, knowing she wouldn't be here for that, yet the thought fled as he covered her softness with his mouth. She cried out, instant heat speeding through her, making her shiver and moan.

"I love your taste," he murmured, and brought her body to an incredible peak in seconds. Suddenly he stood and pushed her against the tiled wall, lifted her and plunged into her slick depths.

"Oh, mercy!"

"Nah, no mercy," he said, and thrust hard. "We've years to make up, baby. Years."

"And you plan to do it in one weekend?"

"It would take a lifetime." He withdrew and pushed into her again. "And even that wouldn't be enough."

Hayley gazed into his eyes as he loved her, and she

wondered how she would ever be able to leave him and go back to her career now that she'd had a taste of life with him. She clutched him, hiding her sudden sorrow in the bend of his shoulder. And praying for more time.

Nash had to feed and water the stock, but he wasn't gone twenty minutes when the doorbell rang. When Hayley opened it, a uniformed express-mail carrier stood there offering an envelope. She signed for it and realized it was for her. With a sigh, she walked into the kitchen and took a seat at the table. The envelope contained her bills, forwarded through Katherine, ever since she'd given up her apartment in Georgia when her internship was done. She opened the envelope and went first to her tuition loan. Would she ever pay it off? The bank had lent her only a small portion, and because she'd held numerous jobs to pay for her survival and some of the tuition as it came, she didn't have any other collateral to put against the borrowing. Her car, faithful Lurlene, wasn't worth more than five hundred dollars and was useless for barter. She'd had to wager future earnings as a physician. The pressure of it hit her again, as it did whenever she had time to think about it. She rubbed the spot between her eyes. It made her see how little she had and how empty her life had become. Bills and a broken-down car, her furniture stuck in storage at Kat's. Not much for a woman her age, she thought.

She glanced around the spacious kitchen and sighed. She was going to miss being in this house, and her throat tightened. The buzzer on the dryer sounded and she pushed off the stool, heading into the laundry room to finish folding the last load. She pulled out a little pink T-shirt, smoothing the still-warm sleeves, then brought it to her nose, inhaling deeply. A pair of iden-

tical faces loomed in her mind. Kate, bright and ener-
getic, slightly tomboyish. And Kim, a little shy, cau-
tious and very much a girl. So alike yet so different.
She missed them, remembering them playing dress-up,
dancing with her.

The ring of the phone jolted her, and she scrambled
for it.

"Hi, Miss Hayley."

"Kate! Hi, honey!"

"How come you always know which one of us it is?
Even Grandma doesn't."

Oh, how she wanted to hold this child right now.
"Must be a doctor thing."

Kate giggled on the other end.

"What's up?"

"We rode Bullet and Peso today."

"I take it those are horses."

"Yeah." She giggled again.

A click on the phone and Kim's voice burst through.
"Miss Hayley, Kate jumped."

Hayley straightened. "You did what!"

"You weren't supposed to tell, Kimmy."

"But you did it, Kate!"

Jumping a horse! Good Lord, Hayley thought. "What
did Grandma say?"

"Grandma taught me," Kate said as if she should
know.

Hayley groaned. "Does your father know you do this
sort of thing?"

"Uh-huh."

"Beg pardon?"

"Yes, ma'am."

"Well, then, that's great. Mercy me, Kate, I'm so

proud of you! I can barely sit in the saddle without having to hold on for dear life.''

"Oh, Daddy can teach you, Miss Hayley. It's not hard."

Hayley's gaze fell on the stack of bills, the check Katherine had enclosed barely making a dent in her debts. She didn't want to say that she wasn't going to be around to learn and just kept the conversation going. Before she said goodbye, she told them their father was still working and she'd have him call them. When she clicked off, Hayley hugged the phone to her chest, her eyes burning. When she finally put it back on the wall bracket, tears were falling fast down her cheeks. She loved Nash, loved his children, his home, but she didn't think she could do it all—career, home and family. Oh, she knew there were women out there who managed quite well, but Hayley didn't have anything to go by. She hadn't had a stable life since college and before that, it was town to town and school to school, always leaving what few friends she'd made behind. She'd be busy in the next three years and too far away to make it work. Nash and the girls deserved better. They deserved a full-time wife and mother.

Days of loneliness loomed ahead. No sweet smiles in the morning. No strong man making her feel protected and cherished. Being a doctor didn't mean very much without someone to share her nights with, she realized. But she wasn't used to handing her burdens to anyone. It was scary to give yourself into someone else's care, to depend on them for your happiness. She'd done that once and gotten burned so badly she'd never recovered.

Dropping to the stool and bracing her elbows on the counter, she covered her face and tried not to cry, tried not to miss Nash and the twins already. She struggled to remember that she had obligations to St. Anthony's Hospital, and that they were expecting her to take care of the sick and wounded. What good was a doctor who couldn't take care of herself and her own breaking heart? she thought.

Nash stopped in the front hall, catching a glimpse of her through the kitchen to where she sat at the counter. His chest clenched. She was crying. He loved her so much, but the inevitable still hovered like a dark cloud, threatening their happiness. He didn't want to see her so miserable. It hurt him that he might be pushing her without even realizing it. But he couldn't help it. He wanted her, and deep inside he wanted her to put him before her damned career.

Her quiet sobs came to him, driving their torment deeper. He cursed timing and circumstances and her stubbornness that kept them from a future. And he decided that he needed to do something about it and fast. Time was getting away from them.

That night Nash made her forget. He showered her with attention, offering her champagne and chocolate-dipped strawberries, feeding her himself and playing games with the dark chocolate and then swimming naked with her in the pool. He make love to her under the midnight stars until she was breathless and begging him to stop. And then he loved her some more. He held her all night, unable to sleep for a secret feeling that if he did, she'd be gone when he awoke.

Hayley walked the long corridor of the barn. "Okay, boss-man. Horses are watered, that ornery stallion is prancing like a king in the paddock, and the chickens are fed. What next?"

"Wanna roll in the hay?" Nash said as she approached him. He tossed a forkful of hay into the stall.

She propped her shoulder on the wall and regarded him. Snug-fitting jeans showed off his trim hips, and that black T-shirt stretching over his muscled chest made her want to strip him naked and play with all that man lying beneath. But since the ranch hands had the day off, they had chores to do first.

She cocked her head and gave him a saucy smile. "You just want to ride something else besides a horse."

He grinned. "Now there's a thought." He bent and kissed her, snaking his arm around her and pulling her flush against him.

"I still have the pigs to feed."

His brow knitted. "Be careful," he warned.

"I'll just toss the grub and run."

He smiled, pecked her cheek, then let her go. "Git, then. I have plans for you later."

"Something I might enjoy?" She stepped toward the entrance.

He looked her over, long and hot. "So far you have."

"Arrogant cuss."

"That's not what you said this morning."

She blushed. She'd awoken this morning from a fantastically erotic dream, aroused and hungry for him, and realized just as he'd pushed his body into hers that it wasn't a dream. "You took the advantage," she said.

"Guilty, darlin' guilty," he replied without remorse. "You lying next to me, all bare and rosy, was too much of a temptation."

Hayley was tempted to strip right then and there and tempt him again, since he looked so on edge. His eyes smoldered and her body pulsed with life. "How much longer?" she found herself asking.

"Another hour maybe."

She glanced at her watch. "Meet me on the veranda for lunch?"

His gaze slid over her. "I ought to be mighty hungry by then."

"I wasn't talking about food."

"Neither was I."

Laughing, she dashed out of the barn and headed to the pig sty. Threatening to make them into pork chops, she fed the beasts, then returned to the house. After a quick dip in the pool to cool off, she showered and slipped into gauzy dark blue slacks and a loose blouse. She looked forward to spending the day with him, and after running a load of laundry, she prepared lunch and waited.

And waited.

Frowning at the time, she walked through the house, calling to him, and getting no answer, she left the house. Halfway to the barn, she heard a strange howl. She ran to the breeding barn, her bare feet slapping on the concrete floor.

She found him in a sanitized-looking stall with a mare. The animal's belly was full and moving, and Hayley realized, she was about to give birth. The fourth one since she'd arrived.

"Okay," she said. "I forgive you for being late. Want me to call the vet?"

He didn't glance up. "Already did. She's on her way, but there's no time." He looked up at her. "I need your help, honey."

She blinked at him, then the horse. "You're kidding, right?"

He shook his head. "Come on, baby, you're a doc. You can do this."

She stepped into the stall, grabbing a heavy vinyl apron to cover her clothes. "Tell me what to do."

"My hands are too big and she needs help."

Hayley nodded and knelt to examine the horse. "A hoof is caught and it's going to tear the uterus."

"That's what I was afraid of. Damn. I'd hate to lose this one."

It was a half-million-dollar horse, Hayley knew, and for a second she wondered if Nash cared about the expense or the animal. Then she saw him stroke the mare, whisper to her in soft cooing tones and she knew better.

"Let me see if I can…" She rolled back her sleeves and shoved her arm up the birth canal. A few tense seconds passed before she latched onto the hoof and followed the line of it. Her lips pinched in concentration, she adjusted the foal as best she could.

In the distance came the sound of a car and then a door slamming.

"Mr. Rayburn," a female voice called seconds later.

Nash hailed the vet, and Hayley was just pulling her arm free when she stepped into the stall. The vet knelt and Nash introduced Dr. Janna McLean to Hayley as she checked the animal.

Hayley went to the sink and washed up as the vet took over.

"Okay, Belle," the vet said to the horse. "You're doing fine. The rest is up to you." She palpated the horse's stomach, glancing between the pair, her gaze ending on Hayley. "Nice to meet you. You're the talk of the town, you know."

Hayley frowned as Janna checked the animal's breathing. "No, I didn't. How so?"

The vet laughed, but kept her gaze on her work.

"Every woman in two counties has been doing her best to get Nash's attention for years."

"I had his attention years ago," Hayley said with a glance at Nash. "So I guess I had an advantage."

"That and the fact that I've always loved her," Nash said.

Hayley's breath caught. Saying it to her was one thing; saying it aloud to a stranger was quite another. A lump swelled in her throat.

Janna looked up, her gaze again shifting between the two. "And you're not shy about it, either, I see."

"No, ma'am." He leaned toward Hayley, cupped her jaw and kissed her.

"Oh, Nash," she said on a soft moan.

Janna sent them a disgusted look. "Why don't you two get out of here? Belle and I are fine. My assistant should be here any second, and frankly, you two are no help."

Nash looked skeptically between her and one of his prize broodmares.

"I swear. A Scotswoman's honor," Janna said, grinning.

Hayley walked to the entrance. On his knees near the horse, Nash hesitated. Janna gave him a shove. "Go," she said in a low voice. "From what I hear, she's leaving soon, so go."

Did everyone know their business? he wondered as he stood and followed Hayley. She hadn't made it out of the barn yet when Nash swept his arm around her waist and walked with her toward the house. Behind them, Janna's assistant sped up the drive.

"Lunch is probably spoiled."

He frowned at her, then tipped her head back to look her in the eye.

"Out with it."

She sighed and laid her head on the crook of his shoulder. "Nothing, really. I miss the girls, I guess."

Liar, he thought, and knew what she was thinking. Leaving. The thought speared his chest painfully and he gripped her a little more tightly. As they walked through the front doors, he led her into the formal dining room. She was still looking down and he nudged her. She looked at him, and the sadness in her eyes made him bleed inside. He nodded toward the table.

Hayley's breath caught. On the center of the table wrapped with a big blue ribbon was a black medical bag. She stepped away from him and reached for the card.

I knew you could do it, it said.

Her eyes filled with tears. "Thank you, darlin', but I thought you resented my career."

His brows shot up in surprise. "Heck no, honey. I grew up. You don't resent mine, do you?"

"No."

He stepped close and slid his arms around her waist. "I'm so proud of you. Not many people have your determination."

"You mean stubbornness."

"That too," he said with a smile.

His finger traced her temple. "I love you, Hayley. I want a future with you. God, you have to know that by now."

"I guess I do." Her gaze searched his. "It's just too much right now, and it's not fair to you or the girls."

"Are you refusing to even consider it?"

"No, no," she cried softly. "But I'm talking three years."

"It's been seven and my feelings for you haven't

changed. They've only grown stronger." His gaze darkened with frustration and disappointment. "I thought it was the same for you, but I guess I was wrong."

"No, you weren't," she was quick to say.

He couldn't hide the anger in his voice when he said, "Then maybe you're just too damn scared to let me in and really share a life with you." Nash reached for the medical bag. "I know what I want, Hayley."

He spun the bag around and walked away.

When he closed his office door behind him, Hayley dragged her gaze to the medical bag. There was a brass nameplate that read *Hayley Albright Rayburn, MD.*

Twelve

Nash stirred and reached for her, but he found the space beside him cold and empty. He sat up, rubbing his hand over his hair and looking around. Hayley wasn't here. He knew things weren't solved between them, especially after she'd stayed away from him most of the night, but when she slipped into his bed and made love with him, he thought at least they still had a chance to smooth the edges.

Throwing back the covers, he dressed and headed for the door, flinging it open. His heart slammed to his stomach when he saw the suitcase in the foyer.

He called to her. No response, so he went to her room, then the kitchen. He found her sitting at the table, staring into her coffee cup.

"What the hell is that?" He flung his hand in the direction of the suitcase.

"I got a call this morning. I'm needed at St. Anthony's this week. Tomorrow, in fact."

"You were going to leave without saying goodbye?"

"No."

"Bull."

Her gaze jerked up. "Please don't make this harder, Nash."

"Dammit, Hayley, I will make it harder. You're leaving me."

Her heart cracked, a piece falling away as each moment passed. She tried to sip her coffee and found she couldn't swallow, so she set it aside.

She stood. "See this?" She shoved the envelope she'd received yesterday across the table. "I'm obligated. I wagered my future as a doctor, my salary, and now it's time to pay the bills."

"I could take care of that in a heartbeat."

"I don't want you to. It's not your career, it's mine!"

"That's what sharing a life is all about. We give what the other needs."

"Well, I wouldn't know about sharing, Nash, since I've been alone most of my life."

"We can change that."

"Not now, we can't! I signed a contract. I have to go!" Her lip trembled and tears spilled. "Please don't fight me on this."

"I love you."

"I love you, too, but it's not enough and you deserve better."

"Are you telling me to go find someone else who will stay in the kitchen? For pity's sake, Hayley, do you really think that's how I see a wife?" He plowed his fingers through his hair. "You're not giving us a chance."

She shook her head, backing away. "Don't say it. Please don't. You know I can't think that far ahead and it's mean." An invisible fist squeezed her heart. The other night at the ball he'd revealed his true feelings, and the declaration of "all or nothing" told her how little she could give and how much he wanted. Being here a moment longer, she'd weaken and later regret it. She had just as much at risk. And her look told him a proposal did not fix anything between them.

He was staring at the bills when he heard her heavy shuddering sigh. He glanced up, but her face was turned away. Her fingers worried the edge of the counter.

Suddenly she moved to the sink, pouring out her coffee and rinsing the cup. She stilled before she put it in the dishwasher. How could such a simple act make her hurt so much? she thought.

He crossed the room and caught her arm. "Baby, don't close me out."

She made a sound, weary and hopeless, but refused to look at him. "I have to. You're the one making demands you know I can't meet."

"That's because I want you to stay. I want you in my life."

She turned on him, her anger rising with the heat in her voice. "*You* want." More tears shimmered in her eyes. "Well, you got what you wanted years ago. You made your choice and I wasn't it. You thought of yourself and duty, and never once thought of me, Nash."

"That's not true." He pushed his fingers through his hair. "God, Hayley, there hasn't been a day that I haven't thought of you."

"Am I supposed to feel sorry for you? 'Cause I don't." She looked away, swallowing. When she spoke again, her voice was strained. "What about what I need now, Nash?'' She faced him. "I'm in your life, in your house, your bed… I love you, I love your children. How much deeper can I get?''

"As deep as I can get you.''

Her expression turned bitter. "That's a lie. You won't let me.'' He looked confused. "I'm trying to be realistic and you keep throwing up barriers. All or nothing, you said at the ball. Well, right now, I can't give you that. So where does that leave us?'' She sniffled, and when he took a step toward her, she backed away. "No, don't touch me.'' If he did, she'd melt into his arms and forget her anger. She wanted it right now. Needed it. "You know, it's just like it was years ago. Your way or the highway.''

"I didn't mean for it to come out like that, but I also know you're scared out of your mind.''

She lifted her chin, staring him down with eyes gone hard as bottle glass. "I've lived my entire life scared, Nash. Scared when my father went off to work that he'd never come back. Scared that when I was a teenager he wouldn't tell me all I needed to know about being a woman and I'd make terrible mistakes. And when he died, I was numb with fear—I was alone. I had no one who'd cared.'' Her eyes burned and she couldn't look at him anymore. She didn't want his pity. She wanted him to understand.

"I cared, baby.''

"Oh, yeah, sure you did,'' she threw at him bitterly. "You cared so much you walked right out of my life and never looked back.''

His expression filled with pain. No wonder she'd let him get only just so close. He'd reinforced her darkest fears.

"Michelle's been gone a long time.'' Her voice was

soft and hurt when she said, "If you loved me so much, how come I never heard from you?"

"I knew you'd gone on with your life, just as I knew you didn't want wounds opened again. Neither did I. We parted badly and I didn't hold out any hope."

She looked at him. "But you never even tried!" she accused.

"No. I didn't. I couldn't." His blue eyes hardened with the tone of his voice. "I have my girls to consider in everything I do, Hayley. They can feel tension when I don't even know it's there. And I knew seeing you again would have been hard on us both." If he'd so much as spent an hour thinking about her, the girls would feel it and say something. "You were my deepest regret."

"And you were mine." She shook her head sadly. "I should have come to you and demanded an explanation. But I thought if you could leave so easily, what we had was only in my imagination."

"It wasn't. I didn't imagine last night and the days before. I love you and I know you love me."

"Of course I do."

"Why are you fighting me, then?"

"Because I don't have a choice."

"We all have choices."

She shook her head, angry with him. "You didn't know a damn thing about who I was years ago and you don't now."

His temper rose and he reached for her hand. "Now there, you're wrong."

She jerked free. "How could you know?" She scoffed. "Look at this place. It's a palace!" She threw her arms wide. "You have the American dream. You're good-looking, rich, powerful, respected and adored by all, plus you have two beautiful children. You've lived in the lap of luxury all your life, and I don't hold it against you, but because of it, you know *nothing* of how I've lived.''

"Dammit, Hayley, my memory isn't that bad.''

"You saw what I wanted you to see, wanted everyone except my sorority sisters to see. Have you ever gone hungry to pay for a class?'' His features yanked taut. "I've lived on nothing but popcorn and caffeine because if my grade point dropped, I'd have lost my scholarships. Then in med school, I held three jobs to make the tuition for the next semester. I was scared I'd never finish my graduate studies and wondered if I was going to be cleaning toilets for the rest of my life because working so hard left me barely enough time to study!''

"But that's over. You did it.'' He approached her, slowly as if she were a frightened animal and would bolt. "What are you so scared of now?''

She didn't answer, her throat choking off her air and making her gasp over and over.

He eased near, touching her chin and tipping her head back. "What, baby?''

Fat tears rolled down her cheek. "I'm terrified that when I finally get my dream and can legally write MD after my name, that it won't be what I'd wanted all along.''

His brow knitted. "How come?''

"To see you again, to love you and love your babies—'' she gripped his upper arms "—it's all I'd wanted with you, everything I lost thrown in my face…and it's still out of my reach.''

Her anguish was a part of him, making him hurt for her, with her, and when he was trying to be patient and let her see what he could offer her, all she saw was what she could have had. Before he'd taken it away from both of them.

"My God, Nash—" she searched his features "—don't you know if I could, I would stay?"

His heart soared with hope. That was all he needed to hear. "Then I'll find a way, baby." His fingers trailed over her cheek, wiping away her tears before sliding into her hair. "I will. I swear it."

At his touch a little whimper escaped her and she closed her eyes, trembling.

"Shh." He bent, his lips near. "I will. Trust me."

She kissed him, a tender trembling kiss filled with want and sorrow.

"I have to go. No. I do, Nash. I do. Don't make me fight for you and my career, please." Oh, how easily she could give up ten years of work when he looked at her like that. "I need you, Nash, but I need this, too. I know I can't have both."

Then he stepped back suddenly, his gaze narrowing. "I'd never stop you, Hayley. And I'm not sure I want a woman who is working all the time and whose career comes before love and family."

Her chin lifted. "I thought family stood by you no matter what. I guess I was wrong."

He paled.

"This is who I am, who I need to be to like myself. I've made the sacrifices, Nash. I'm the one who loses every time. If you can't accept this much, then we can never be together."

She swept past him, picked up her suitcase and walked out of his life.

Nash stared at the empty kitchen, then dropped his head and closed his eyes.

His chest burned so badly he could feel his heart breaking.

Kate and Kim sat on the sofa and stared blankly at the TV, their eyes red from crying. They wouldn't speak to Nash. They blamed him for Hayley leaving and he couldn't fault them.

"Hungry?"

They glared at him.

He sighed and grabbed his hat, striding toward the door when he heard Kate say, "She forgot about my tooth."

The hurt in his daughter's voice brought him back into the room. "What?"

"Miss Hayley said the tooth fairy would come twice. Since I live here but lost it at Grandma's."

Nash took a risk and said, "Did you look?"

Kate lifted her gaze.

Nash's heart shattered again at the hurt in her eyes, her curled-down lip so like her sister's. She shook her head. He arched a brow, and when she took off for her room, stomping up the stairs, Nash swore he didn't move a muscle till she came back down. She showed him the silver dollar, and something twisted inside Nash.

Leave it to Hayley not to forget anyone else but herself, he thought.

"I'm never going to spend it."

Nash sighed and knelt, aware of his mother and Mrs. Winslow standing in the dining-room doorway. "Honey, Hayley is a doctor and she has to do this for three years."

"Did you make her go, Daddy?"

His throat closed. "I wanted her to stay, honey, but

she had to leave. You knew that from the start.'' And so did he, he realized.

Kim walked up beside her sister. ''Do something, Daddy. Make her come back.'' Her blue eyes filled with tears.

''I can't.'' He hugged them and they sobbed in his arms. Nash picked them up and sat down on the couch with them. He cursed Hayley and her stubborn pride, and cursed himself for not seeing a way to fix this.

The girls, having cried through the night, fell asleep, and he covered them and stood, walking into the kitchen. Mrs. Winslow stepped into the laundry room, closing the door behind her as Nash lifted his gaze to his mother.

''I thought I raised a smarter son.''

''What do you want me to do, Mom? Leave the ranch to Jake and go live in Savannah?''

''Hayley is so far in debt, Nash, she can't even think of stopping for anything, even love. She needs you more now.''

''I need her.''

''Then do something about it, for pity's sake.''

''What?''

''Get her home.''

Nash dug the heels of his palms into his eyes and sighed. ''Don't you think I've tried? I did everything but lay a red carpet before her.''

''Money isn't everything. Telling her what you can offer her is different from making it happen. And you're a fool to think she should put her residency on hold, especially when she's still paying for that tuition. She's honor bound to those obligations first. And your time with Michelle ought to tell you that honor and duty can make a person do some stupid things.''

His features tightened.

"She's sacrificed more than you and I could ever imagine to get where she is. A life together isn't always fifty-fifty. You need to give a little more."

I've made the sacrifices, Nash, she'd said. *I'm the one who loses every time.*

Nash stared without really seeing, then grabbed his hat, jamming it on as he strode out the front door.

Grace raced after him. "What are going to do?"

"Bring my woman home," he said, and climbed into his truck.

Grace smiled. "That's my boy," she whispered as he drove away in a cloud of dust.

Nash found her on the maternity ward, wearing blue scrubs and looking every inch the doctor she was. A nurse stood near, waiting for her to finish writing on a chart.

"Hayley." Her head jerked up, her gaze slamming into his. The chart faltered in her grip.

"Nash." She swallowed, absently handing the chart to the nurse. "What are you doing here?"

He glanced at the people lingering, then walked to her. He stopped a few feet from her, his arms fairly throbbing to hold her. "Can we talk?"

Hayley gazed up at him, the pain of being apart filling with her love for him. She nodded and gestured to the empty waiting room. Then she faced him.

"You don't look so hot," he said. She looked sad and exhausted, dark circles beneath her eyes, and she was thinner.

"Neither do you." She was about to sweep his hair off his brow, then decided it was best not to touch him. But, oh, how she missed him.

He took a step closer and tossed his hat on a chair. When he spoke his voice was low and raspy. "I can't go on like this."

"Nash—"

"No, let me just say what I have to say." He drew a breath. "The girls are miserable. I'm no good to anyone and the plantation isn't the same, honey."

"I can't come back. You know it." Her eyes stung and she blinked. "What do you want from me? To give up my career that I've worked for all these years to have? You said yourself you need someone there for you and the girls. I can't give you that."

Tears filled her eyes and spilled.

"I can give it all to you, honey."

She shook her head. "It's my debt and my problem."

He reached out and brushed her hair off her forehead. "Baby, you've been on your own for so long you don't know how to let someone else take part of the burden. Let me show you. Let me be the one. Trust me not to hurt you and to do what we have to so we can be together."

Hayley felt as if she was teetering on the edge. *Do it, let him,* a voice chanted. *Share with him.* She'd been utterly miserable for the past few days and could barely concentrate for the sound of her breaking heart. She'd never given anyone her troubles. She'd never had the chance, and it just wasn't in her to spread her problems or ask another to take them.

"I've made some changes so you don't have to give up a thing."

Her brows tightened. "What did you do?"

"I paid off your loans. No," he said when she tried to speak, "just listen. Let me do this. It puts us a step closer. Or don't you love me?"

"Yes, I do," she whispered. "I love you so much it's killing me to look at you."

He sighed, his lips curving for an instant. "That's one thing out of the way. Now I know you have to do your residency, but who says it has to be here?"

"What do you mean?" Her heart started to pound.

"I spoke to the head of this hospital and chief of medicine at the County Hospital in Aiken. They agreed. You can do your residency there. They have the best OB/GYN in the state, if that's what you need. And you can work with Dr. Swanson at his practice. He's retiring in two years and he wants you to think seriously about taking over his patients then."

Hayley couldn't speak. She could be a country doctor and be with Nash. She had the urge to suddenly pinch herself. He'd said to trust him, that he'd find a way, and until this moment, she didn't think anyone could move so many mountains. And never for her.

When she didn't say anything, Nash moved within an inch of her, his tall form crowding her. "I'm not doing this for control or for any other reason than I love you and I need you. I lost you once because I couldn't see how important being a doctor was to you. And all you wanted was a little time. I'm not about to make the same mistake again. I love you, Hayley. I have since I met you. I'm doing this because I can't survive without you." He took her hand, pulling it to his lips. "Marry me."

"Marry us, Miss Hayley."

She turned sharply and found the twins standing near the glass doors.

Nash still held her hand, and when she looked back, he slid a diamond ring on her finger.

The water-clear stones took her breath away.

"You belong with us. Marry us poor lonely Rayburns, sprite. Make us a family."

Nash stared, waiting, his breath locked in his lungs.

Hayley choked out a sob, then another, throwing her arms around his neck and whispering, "Yes, yes!"

The girls cheered and flew to them, their little arms wrapping around Nash and Hayley's legs.

Nash crushed her, squeezing his eyes shut, relief and rapture enveloping him. "Oh, honey," he rasped. "You don't know how you saved me."

Hayley smiled against the curve of his throat, her happy sobs mixing with the sweet joy spinning through her. She did know. His love rescued her, kept her hope alive, and when she let her fingers sink into Kim and Kate's hair, her heart swelled tenfold. Oh, yes. She had it all, every dream she'd had as a kid, as a grown woman trying to find a spot where she belonged. Here it was, in Nash's arms, in Nash's heart.

She was truly a happy woman. How could she not be?

Her family was here.

Epilogue

Five years later

Nash strode down the hospital corridor, his son tucked under his arm and squirming to be let down. His daughters trailed behind him, their heels clicking on the quiet ward floor like the tap of a small hammer. He paused, glanced back and let his gaze drop meaningfully to their boots. They tiptoed the rest of the way down the hall.

He stopped before an office door, knocking, then swinging Alexander across his shoulder. The boy giggled and kicked his feet, nearly catching Nash in the jaw.

Hayley swung around as Nash strode in and dropped Alexander into the patient chair before her desk.

"You're not ready," he said as if he'd known. He crossed to kiss her, a deep kiss of strong love as he slipped his arm around her waist.

"Oh, I needed that," she said on a moan.

"There's more where that came from," he murmured, giving her a devilish smile.

She glanced past him to their children. Alexander was investigating the desk drawer, and Kate caught him before he made it to the supply cabinets. "Do I have to make a date to get some privacy with you?"

"Let's wear 'em out," he said.

She smiled. "Deal. I just have to get these notes down." He let her go, and turning away, she spoke into the Dictaphone as she shrugged out of her lab coat, then opened her closet and pulled out something to wear.

"Mom, come on. We'll be late!"

Hayley glanced at the twins. They looked so cute in their riding outfits. So adult. "I'm hurrying. Close the door." The girls stepped inside and Hayley finished her dictation, switched off the machine, then slipped behind the patient screen.

"Are you ready for this?" He asked, peering around the screen and watching her slip out of her dress. Nash admired her body and wanted to get his hands on all that skin. Her breasts were fuller, her hips a little rounder, but she still turned him on like a floodlight.

"No." She pulled on jeans and a blouse.

"Me, neither. Alexander, simmer down," Nash said with a stern look at his son when the child bounced in Hayley's desk chair. Alexander settled and smiled at him, and Nash's heart overflowed love for his son.

"I tell myself that they are trained and ready, but I just keep remembering the grown men I've put back together after a rodeo."

"Don't worry, Mom," Kate said, and Hayley's heart jerked just as it did every time the twins called her that.

Hayley pulled on her boots. "Not in the mom manual. If fact, it's required." She swiped on some lipstick and ran a brush through her hair before stuffing her clothes in a duffel. She slipped around the screen.

"We promise not to get hurt," Kim said.

Hayley smiled. "That's what you said the last time. Just do your best and you'll be fine."

Handing Nash the duffel, she lifted Alex in her arms, kissed him noisily, then grabbed the black medical bag from the high shelf before heading to the door.

The family filed out, trotting down the hall. Hayley paused to give last-minute instructions to the nurse on duty, then signed out, hoping tomorrow at her offices would be less hectic than at the hospital.

"Got your beeper? Your cell phone?" Nash asked, and she smiled. She could never survive without him. He was truly her partner.

"Good luck, girls," the staff called, and the twins thanked them, then took their little brother from their mother and raced toward the elevators.

Hayley sagged against Nash.

He pressed his lips to the top of her head. "Tired?"

"No, not really." She tipped her head to look at him. "How can I live in the same house with you and still miss you?"

"Auction season, baby, and—" he lowered his voice "—I plan to change that tonight."

Hayley smiled and paused at the elevator doors to kiss him.

"Mom," Kim called, hitching Alexander on her hip. "Put a fire under it."

Hayley grinned, and she and Nash dashed into the elevator before the doors closed.

* * *

"Oh, you're hired, sir," she moaned as his hands massaged over her naked spine, fingers digging deep.

Nash chuckled. Didn't she know how much pleasure it gave him to see her relaxed and happy?

"I did something today."

That long bubble bath was having its effect. "You're doing it now, or do you mean screaming like a madman when your daughter took that jump? Or when she won first place and you bought the entire team dinner?"

Nash grinned, bending down to nibble her neck. "I hired a chef and another housekeeper."

"I was going to get to that," she said, waving limply. Mrs. Winslow had resigned a week ago, and Hayley had barely enough time to interview a replacement.

"I called Katherine."

"Smart man."

"I did it so I could get you alone and ravish you."

"Like I said, smart man." She rolled over, pulling him down on top of her. Her hands were on him, stroking him, arousing him, and Nash didn't think there was a purer moment in his life than when Hayley made love with him.

"I love you," she said between kisses.

"Oh, darlin', that's what I live for."

He made love to her softly, slowly, but the passion rose and spread through them, burning their love deeper with every joining.

Sometime later Nash sank into the huge bed, pulling her close and kissing her again and again. "I've missed my wife." Under the sheets his hand mapped her lush figure.

"I know, and I'm taking some time off." His brows rose. "There're two new residents and we're getting another doctor at the hospital. And I deserve it."

He smiled, and she shifted half over him, her hands folded on his chest, her chin on her wrists.

His brows worked. "What?"

"I'm pregnant."

A grin split his face. Then it froze at her next words.

"And it's twins." His surprise made her laugh and pop up to kiss him. "It's your chromosomes that keep doing that."

He chuckled, squeezing her, then pushed her hair off her face and gazed into her eyes. "Babies," was all he could manage.

Hayley's eyes teared up a little. He saw every moment as she did, a gift of the sweetest kind. He was a strong man, taking care of all of them and giving her more than anyone had a right to have. She loved him with every breath she took, for the man who fought to love her, who shared her burdens and her bed and brought her what she'd missed in her life, a place to belong, a family to love and a heart filled with so much joy there wasn't any room for pain.

"Good thing we have jobs, huh?"

He laughed. "Guess we need to hire a nanny, too."

"No way. That's where all the fun is. That and loving you."

His expression was poignantly tender, and he kissed her, chanting his love and how happy he was that they were going to have more Rayburns to love and he hoped they looked just like her.

With her nestled in his arms, Nash sighed, letting the news fill him and her love surround him. He could barely remember being without her, how lonely he'd been, how lost. The road was wide open now, a welcoming path for more happiness, more love, and though their life felt like a nonstop ride since they'd married,

Nash was enjoying every hectic moment. Especially when the days ended like this, his arms wrapped around his redheaded princess of River Willow.

* * * * *

SILHOUETTE
DESIRE ®

AVAILABLE FROM 15TH JUNE 2001

THE RETURN OF ADAMS CADE BJ James

Adams Cade had returned to face his family-and his childhood love –
Eden Claibourne. Could Eden convince him that his true home was in
her arms?

SLOW WALTZ ACROSS TEXAS Peggy Moreland

Clayton Rankin was convinced that he didn't need anyone. But when
his wife, Rena, told him he was about to lose her, he was determined
to win back her love!

RANCHER'S PROPOSITION Anne Marie Winston

Body & Soul

He'd wanted a woman to share his household duties – not his bed!
But when Lyn Hamill came to work for Cal McCall, he began to
rethink. Cal was determined to make her his wife in *every* way…

SHEIKH'S TEMPTATION Alexandra Sellers

Sons of the Desert

They'd spent an electrifying, passionate night together. But Sheikh
Arash Khosravi had risked his fortune to save his country. Could he
keep Lana when he had nothing to offer her but himself?

THE DETERMINED GROOM Kate Little

Laurel Sutherland needed financial help and Connor Northrup was
the only man who would help her. He had a plan to save the woman
he'd never been able to forget: he was proposing marriage.

THE BABY GIFT Susan Crosby

The Baby Bank

The very pregnant woman standing in front of him couldn't remember
who she was, but Gina Banning was the one woman JT Ryker would
always remember. What he needed to know now was why she'd driven
all this way to see him?

0601/22a

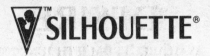

SILHOUETTE

DESIRE®

is proud to present

Sons of the Desert
by
Alexandra Sellers

*Powerful sheikhs born to rule
and destined to find love as
eternal as the sands...*

Sheikh's Temptation July 2001

Sheikh's Honour September 2001

Sheikh's Woman November 2001

0601/SH/LC17

FREE

2 BOOKS

AND A SURPRISE GIFT!

We would like to take this opportunity to thank you for reading this Silhouette® book by offering you the chance to take TWO more specially selected titles from the Desire™ series absolutely FREE! We're also making this offer to introduce you to the benefits of the Reader Service™—

- ★ FREE home delivery
- ★ FREE monthly Newsletter
- ★ FREE gifts and competitions
- ★ Exclusive Reader Service discounts
- ★ Books available before they're in the shops

Accepting these FREE books and gift places you under no obligation to buy; you may cancel at any time, even after receiving your free shipment. Simply complete your details below and return the entire page to the address below. *You don't even need a stamp!*

YES! Please send me 2 free Desire books and a surprise gift. I understand that unless you hear from me, I will receive 4 superb new titles every month for just £2.80 each, postage and packing free. I am under no obligation to purchase any books and may cancel my subscription at any time. The free books and gift will be mine to keep in any case.

DIZEC

Ms/Mrs/Miss/Mr ....Initials..
BLOCK CAPITALS PLEASE

Surname...

Address...

....

....Postcode ....

Send this whole page to:
UK: FREEPOST CN81, Croydon, CR9 3WZ
EIRE: PO Box 4546, Kilcock, County Kildare (stamp required)